BITTER END

Clint knew what Sam's intentions were. The fact that a gun was still gripped in Sam's hand at the moment only drove that point home like a nail in a coffin.

The look on Sam's face was a mix of cocky arrogance and grim satisfaction. He'd finally gotten Clint to stop and listen. He was also about to take the gamble that so many other would-be gunfighters only dreamed of.

Clint stood his ground without making a move. It wasn't his way to back down, but he was never one to pick a fight.

The fight came to him when Sam's hand clenched around his pistol and brought the gun up in a quick snap. His finger squeezed the trigger as he was taking aim, but Clint's hand had already snapped into motion as well.

In one fluid movement, Clint drew the modified Colt and took his shot.

THE GUNSMITH

284

SCORPION'S TALE

J. R. ROBERTS

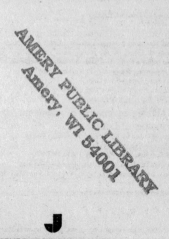

JOVE BOOKS, NEW YORK

THE BERKLEY PUBLISHING GROUP
Published by the Penguin Group
Penguin Group (USA) Inc.
375 Hudson Street, New York, New York 10014, USA
Penguin Group (Canada), 10 Alcorn Avenue, Toronto, Ontario M4V 3B2, Canada
(a division of Pearson Penguin Canada Inc.)
Penguin Books Ltd., 80 Strand, London WC2R 0RL, England
Penguin Group Ireland, 25 St. Stephen's Green, Dublin 2, Ireland (a division of Penguin Books Ltd.)
Penguin Group (Australia), 250 Camberwell Road, Camberwell, Victoria 3124, Australia
(a division of Pearson Australia Group Pty. Ltd.)
Penguin Books India Pvt. Ltd., 11 Community Centre, Panchsheel Park, New Delhi—110 017, India
Penguin Group (NZ), Cnr. Airborne and Rosedale Roads, Albany, Auckland 1310, New Zealand
(a division of Pearson New Zealand Ltd.)
Penguin Books (South Africa) (Pty.) Ltd., 24 Sturdee Avenue, Rosebank, Johannesburg 2196,
South Africa

Penguin Books Ltd., Registered Offices: 80 Strand, London WC2R 0RL, England

This is a work of fiction. Names, characters, places, and incidents either are the product of the author's imagination or are used fictitiously, and any resemblance to actual persons, living or dead, business establishments, events, or locales is entirely coincidental.

SCORPION'S TALE

A Jove Book / published by arrangement with the author

PRINTING HISTORY
Jove edition / August 2005

ISBN: 0-515-13988-2

JOVE®
Jove Books are published by The Berkley Publishing Group,
a division of Penguin Group (USA) Inc.,
375 Hudson Street, New York, New York 10014.
JOVE is a registered trademark of Penguin Group (USA) Inc.
The "J" design is a trademark belonging to Penguin Group (USA) Inc.

PRINTED IN THE UNITED STATES OF AMERICA

10 9 8 7 6 5 4 3 2 1

ONE

It had been a hard summer. Actually, Clint could think of plenty other summers that had been worse than this one, but it was that time of year when the season was wearing out its welcome. The heat had been hanging in the air for long enough that it was getting hard to recall much else. As the breeze started to grow cooler, the change felt so good on Clint's face that it made the last few months seem unbearable by comparison.

This change had seemed even more drastic since Clint had pointed the nose of his Darley Arabian stallion north and snapped the reins. That had been a few weeks ago, and the pair had been headed that way ever since.

Each day, the seasons had been changing around him just as one campsite had been farther north than the one before it. Considering the fact that he'd started his ride in west Texas and now found himself roaming through northern Colorado, those were powerful changes indeed. Clint had a soft spot for Texas, but that wasn't a place known for its beautiful autumns. At this time of year, riding from Texas into Colorado was like crossing over into another world.

The wind tossed Clint's hair and ruffled Eclipse's mane. The Darley Arabian seemed to enjoy the cool mountain air

1

as well, and ran like he had sails when a particularly big gust swept him up. Having just recovered from a nasty little injury, Eclipse was running faster and stronger each day. The doctor in Labyrinth had done a fine job of tending to Eclipse's wound. All the stallion needed now was to stretch his legs.

Stretching his legs was a bit of an understatement for riding up through a major portion of the entire country. Even so, Eclipse seemed to be enjoying every second of it, and Clint was doing the same.

There was something about spending his days doing nothing but roaming over the open trail that hit Clint on an almost primal level. There was nothing better than getting some dust into his lungs and some ground under his boots to clear his mind. The Rocky Mountains had remained in his sight for about a week now, and it was a sight that never seemed to get old.

Every morning, he would climb into his saddle after breaking camp and point to a summit. "That's where we're headed," Clint would say to Eclipse once he saw the stallion glancing in the proper direction. After that, he would snap the reins and hang on as Eclipse did his level best to try and get to the proper spot.

But no matter how hard they rode or how far into the nighttime hours they went, they never seemed to get any closer to the spot where Clint had pointed. Those Rockies were like giants who moved slowly away while Clint kept riding toward them.

Of course, this wasn't Clint's first time through the Rocky Mountains. He knew only too well that those same giants could creep up all too quickly and loom overhead like a weight that was set to drop at any moment. No matter how breathtakingly beautiful they were, those mountains were to be respected. Anyone who didn't know that simple fact would more than likely wind up dead and buried within some lonely pass.

Clint wasn't intent on reaching the mountains on any given day. His interest in them was merely as a spectator, and it was more than enough to bask in the cold winds that blew in off those snowcapped peaks. The ice-chilled water trickling down from the mountain streams was all the reason he needed to keep riding and enjoy the transition from one season to another.

It was late afternoon, but the fading light in the sky made it feel more like early evening. Clint still needed some time to adjust to the dwindling amount of daylight hours, which made him shake his head as he pulled Eclipse to a stop so he could check his watch.

"It's not as late as I thought," he mused. "Still, it feels like it's going to be a cold night."

As he said that, Clint felt a powerful wind tear across the trail and through every bone in his body. Eclipse let out a huffing whinny while shaking his head and stomping his front hooves against the packed earth.

Clint turned up the collar of his jacket and breathed into his hands before rubbing them together. When he lowered his hands, he pulled in a breath that brought with it something else that caught his attention.

Besides the normal scents that came with being so close to the mountains, he picked up a trace of smoke as well as the enticing aroma of brewing coffee. Although he could brew a decent pot of coffee himself, the smell Clint caught now easily put his to shame.

"What do you say, boy?" Clint asked while reaching out to pat Eclipse's neck. "You think whoever's brewing that coffee wouldn't mind sparing a cup?"

Judging by the way he fidgeted, Eclipse's only desire was to get moving and get some more blood flowing through his veins. The Darley Arabian's breaths were starting to come out of its nostrils in gouts of steam.

"Tell you what. If I get some of that coffee in me, I'll be just as raring to go as you are and then we can have a good run before making camp. I'm pretty sure there's a town not too far from here, so maybe we can both bed down somewhere other than the gr—"

Clint's words were cut off by a familiar rumble that rode along the wind just like the scent of coffee had moments ago. This time, however, Clint wasn't quite as happy to receive the message.

"Was that a gunshot?" he whispered, even though he knew perfectly well that it was.

The sound had already tapered off to a crackle in the distance, but that didn't make Clint feel any better about it. He took a moment or two to look around and get a rough feel for which direction the sound had come from. Every one of his instincts pointed him straight in the direction he'd already been headed.

"Looks like our coffee brewer's got some bigger problems than me barging in on him. Let's go see if they need a hand."

With that, Clint snapped the reins and rode straight toward the source of that gunfire.

TWO

Arthur Books was only slightly bulkier than a scarecrow and looked just about as rumpled. Long, bony legs extended out from where he sat so the soles of his feet could be warmed by his campfire. The flames crackled beneath a sturdy frame of branches that held a metal pot swinging in the breeze.

The slender fellow's torso was wrapped in no fewer than four coats, not one of which was thick enough to hold back a chill on its own. His face was sprouting a thick bush of a beard and his hair was a tangled mess underneath a floppy old hat.

Hands wrapped in tattered gloves were holding a tin cup with steam rising up over its rim. That steam was fading, however, since the hot liquid inside was quickly draining through the hole that had just been shot through the cup.

Arthur's eyes grew wider as they moved down to look at the bullet hole and his hands started trembling uncontrollably. It took a little while for the facts to reach his brain and then finally sink in. Once that happened, he pitched the cup away and wound up tossing it straight into the fire.

The flames sputtered and spat out some coffee-flavored smoke as Arthur hopped up from where he was sitting. He almost flopped onto his belly as he twisted around and made a hasty grab for the rifle that was laying on the ground nearby.

"I don't think so, Art," came a voice amid the crunch of leaves and branches. The man who'd spoken walked out from the tangle of trees surrounding the camp. The ground was littered with broken twigs as well as a thick carpet of leaves and mulch.

The new arrival stood over Arthur, pointing a Smith and Wesson pistol down at the other man. He looked to be just as filthy as Arthur, but carried it a little better. The dirt just seemed more comfortable on him, as did the wide filthy smile.

"Get up," the other man said. "And leave that rifle right where it's at."

Arthur made his way to his feet, which was no small task considering how much he was shaking. His hands came up to chest level and his mouth gaped open and shut like a fish. "I was . . . I only had . . . I didn't mean . . ."

"Quit yer yammering. What'd he send you?"

"Wh-what did who send me?"

The man's head cocked to one side in an unspoken warning. His gun hand came up just a little while the look in his eyes made it perfectly clear he wouldn't mind pulling the trigger again. "You tryin' to test me?"

"No, of course not, Sam. I wouldn't do something like that."

"Then tell me what he sent you or this gets real ugly."

Arthur took a few tentative steps away from the man. Even as he inched toward the fire, he seemed to be preparing to bolt straight through the flames. His face twitched into a frightened mask, almost as though he knew what the rest of him was about to do and wasn't at all happy about it.

"You kill me," Arthur said in a wavering tone, "and you won't get any of the answers you want."

"So you are trying to test me, huh? Well, first of all, you

might as well forget about trying to run away from me because my boys ain't too far and they'll pick you off like a quail that's been flushed from its nest. Second, I didn't never say I was going to kill you. At least," Sam added while lowering the barrel of his gun until it aimed at Arthur's knee, "not right away."

That sapped what little bit of courage Arthur had managed to build. Not only did he stop moving away from Sam, but he stepped into the same spot where he'd started. "I s-swear. I don't know what you're talking about."

"Then what're you out here for? You're a sorry excuse for a mountain man and you sure as hell ain't no trapper."

"Those are both lucrative trades. Perhaps I was—"

"Cut the bullshit. I ain't in no mood for it. I'll give you till the count of three and then I start making you wish you was dead."

As Arthur's breaths sped up, they came from between his clenched teeth like steam rising from the kettle over the fire. His eyes darted back and forth as his fingers opened and closed into helpless fists.

"One . . ."

Having tethered Eclipse to a tree about fifty yards back, Clint had continued on foot toward the gunshot he'd heard. It turned out that he wasn't as far from the source as he'd thought. The shot had only sounded more distant because it had been muffled by a thick stand of trees.

Those same trees got thicker with each step Clint took within them. On one hand, it made it near impossible to keep his footsteps anything close to silent. On the other hand, there was plenty of places to hide and plenty of other things pushing the leaves around in a noisy, constant rustle.

Before too long, Clint could hear the sound of voices in the distance. Before he got too focused upon that, however, he caught sight of a movement from the corner of his eye that wasn't caused by the wind.

He froze in mid-stride, crouched down with his hand close to the modified Colt holstered at his side. Every one of Clint's senses stretched outward, but it didn't take much to spot the armed man kneeling at the base of a thick, weathered tree trunk. The man was holding a rifle in both hands, using his bent knee to support one arm.

As much as Clint wanted to get behind some better cover, he knew that doing so would only make more noise and draw the armed man's attention. Although he couldn't be certain if that man had been the one to fire the shot that had brought him here, Clint was never too keen on taking risks like that.

Then again, as the rifleman snapped around to take quick aim at Clint, it seemed that the time for taking risks was just getting started.

THREE

Clint ticked away the moments in his head as though a fuse had been lit the moment the rifleman had shifted toward him. Although the moments barely added up to a whole second, every last fraction of that second made a difference.

Mainly, Clint waited until the other man's intentions were clear and he was committed to them. The first part of that equation was easy enough to figure out since the rifleman sighted down his barrel, which was pointed directly at Clint.

When the second part kicked in, Clint felt his blood pulse through his veins with a little extra speed. He launched himself forward using both legs, springing out of the way when he figured it was too late for the rifleman to shift his aim.

The rifle shot cracked through the air, proving Clint's guess to be right as the bullet kicked up a mound of dirt where he'd previously been standing. It was a hell of a way to prove his timing skills, but at least it paid off.

Now that he'd taken his shot, the rifleman needed to find where Clint had gone, readjust his aim, and take another shot. All of that bought Clint enough time to find a thick enough tree to use as protection. Fortunately, there were more than enough trunks to choose from, and Clint pressed his back against a mass of lumber thick enough to stop any bullet.

Without having to think about it, Clint had already drawn the Colt from its holster. The pistol's weight felt just as familiar to him as the weight of his hand at the end of his arm. When he peeked around the side of the tree, the Colt went right along with him.

And when the next rifle shot hissed toward the tree, both Clint and the pistol tucked behind it for safety.

"Damn," Clint snarled under his breath.

The rifleman was a little quicker than he'd thought, but at least Clint was able to learn that without having to spill any blood. Of course, that didn't make his task any easier.

There was always the option of turning around and letting the rifleman shoot at rabbits in peace.

"Help!" came a strained voice from a spot deeper within thê woods.

That voice, along with the shots that continued to be fired at him, made it next to impossible for Clint to leave just yet. He didn't like the thought of turning his back on someone shouting for help. And he sure as hell didn't like being mistaken for a target in a shooting gallery.

"Go on and scream all you want," Sam said. "Only ones that can hear you are probably just gonna laugh about it anyway."

Once he took a moment to catch his breath, Arthur looked around at the woods expectantly. "There were shots."

"Probably just one of the boys shootin' at a bird. Anyway, where were we? Oh, yeah. Two . . ."

"This is ridiculous," Arthur sputtered. "Go ahead and search me. Search the camp. I don't know what else you want from me."

The next word sat poised upon Sam's lips like an arrow nocked against a bowstring. He seemed torn about whether or not he would let the arrow fly or give in to whatever else it was that rattled around inside of him. Finally, he lowered his gun.

Before Sam could do anything else, however, he heard another gunshot. This one wasn't like the others, and that did not set well with him at all. "You got anyone else here with you, Art?"

Arthur's eyes grew wide once again and he shook his head so much that it seemed about ready to twist off his shoulders. "It's just me, I swear!"

"Then who else is shooting?"

"I just asked you that same question."

"I'm sick of playing games. You need to tell me what he sent you and tell me quick because you don't have any time left."

Sucking in every breath and pushing it out again, Arthur was on the verge of keeling over. Still, before he let another word pass his lips, he clenched his mouth shut and averted his eyes.

"All right, then," Sam said, positioning himself like a one-man firing squad. "If that's the way you want to play it."

Clint pulled himself back behind the tree after taking a few shots at the rifleman. He didn't expect to hit anything but trees himself, but at least the shots had given him some breathing room. The rifleman took a moment to rethink his own strategy, allowing the sound of gunfire to bleed off into the cold winds.

Before it could get too quiet, Clint crouched down low and made a quick dash for the closest tree. He was ready to fire or duck down even lower, but neither one was necessary. No shots were fired at him and no movement could be seen.

As soon as he got to the next tree, Clint pressed his back

to it and then peeked around the other side. The new vantage point wasn't drastically different, but it was enough of a change for him to get a look at the rifleman crouching behind his own cover.

Since the last time Clint had seen the rifleman, he'd ducked behind a boulder grown over with a bush and some saplings. That allowed him to remain hidden while laying the rifle over the top of the boulder for support.

Clint reached down for the closest rock he could pick up in one hand. All his fingers came across was dirt and leaves, however, prompting him to curse and take a look down for himself. Sure enough, there wasn't so much as a pebble to be found in arm's reach.

Plucking a bullet from his gun belt, Clint tossed the round toward a spot not too far from where he'd been. The bullet was big enough to make some noise as it hit the ground and that noise was loud enough to draw the rifleman's attention.

Snapping his aim toward the sound, the rifleman squeezed off a quick shot and then levered another round into his chamber.

That gave Clint enough time to launch into a forward roll toward a thick clump of bushes. Rather than stop there, he kept low and rolled through the bushes. When he stopped himself with an outstretched leg, Clint was in a spot at the rifleman's flank.

Although he'd seen this movement from the corner of his eye, the rifleman was already turned in the other direction. He'd tried to draw a bead on Clint, but was unable to get a clear shot until his target was practically behind him.

Laying on his side with his gun arm extended, Clint let a fraction of a second pass before he did anything else. That wasn't a lot of time, but it was more than enough for him to see what the rifleman intended to do next.

By focusing his aim and tensing his trigger finger, the

rifleman made that fraction of a second the last one of his life.

Clint took his shot. The modified Colt bucked against his palm and spat its round through the air to carve a tunnel through the rifleman's head.

Spinning around as though he'd been tossed from a moving wagon, the rifleman snapped his head back and let his gun fall to the ground. He was dead before his back hit the earth, staring up at the sky with unblinking eyes.

By this time, Clint had already moved on.

FOUR

Arthur stared down the barrel of Sam's gun, certain that it was going to be the last thing he'd ever see. His jaw trembled and his heart clenched within his chest. Faced with the possibility of being sent to his Maker, he closed his eyes and lowered his head. It was time to give up what he'd been trying so desperately to keep.

"Sorry to interrupt," came a voice that cut in just before Arthur could spill his guts. "But I don't think you're welcome around here."

Up until this moment, Sam had been settling into his superior position like he would into a well-worn saddle. Even the gunshots crackling around him didn't overly concern him since he knew he would get what he'd come for no matter what else happened. Now, however, that confidence was eroding.

"Who the hell are you?" Sam asked the figure who stepped into the camp from the surrounding trees.

Clint stepped forward, holding the Colt at hip level. Although it wasn't pointed at anyone in particular, it was plain to see that that could be rectified without too much trouble. "I just stopped by because I smelled the coffee brewing," he said. "Seems like not everyone appreciates a good cup as much as I do."

"This ain't none of your business, mister," Sam warned. "You'd best leave before me or my boys decide to make you leave."

"Oh, you must be referring to those fellas I passed on the way in here," Clint said casually. His tone dropped to a deadlier baritone as he added, "They did their best to stop me. Some of them won't be joining you for the ride back."

Sam's eyes narrowed as he shifted on his feet. While his palm started to itch against the handle of his pistol, he recalled the gunshots he'd heard not too long ago. His eyes then snapped to the Colt in Clint's hand. The fact that his boys hadn't busted into the camp by now filled in the rest of the story.

"He a friend of yours?" Sam asked Arthur.

Although he seemed more surprised than anyone else in the vicinity, Arthur nodded vehemently. "I didn't expect to see him just now, but yeah."

Whether or not Sam believed that didn't matter much. All that mattered to him was that whoever this third man was, he wasn't one of his and he'd made it through a screen of riflemen to get to where he was standing at the moment.

As if deciding that Arthur no longer existed, Sam shifted his gaze back over to Clint. "You killed my boys?"

"Not all of them," Clint replied without so much as batting an eye. "Just the ones who refused to admit they held a losing hand."

Sam nodded slowly, digesting what he'd heard. He looked back over to Arthur and gritted his teeth. "So what now? You comin' after me?"

"Only if you want to shoot an unarmed man right in front of me."

"You don't know what any of this is about, mister. Just walk away and leave it be."

"If your business is so important, than you don't need a gun and a band of killers to talk it over. Otherwise, I'll just figure this is a robbery or something worse. Either way, I can't just stand by and watch someone be gunned down in cold blood."

Taking a step back, Sam squared off against Clint as his face took on a new intensity. It seemed as though his features had just frozen over and his eyes had become two hunks of steel wedged in his skull. After making his deliberation, Sam arrived at a decision. Rather than shift his aim toward Clint, he eased the pistol back into its holster.

"You made a good choice," Clint said. "Now you two can talk like civilized men or go your separate ways."

Sam stepped back slowly, measuring each step with the back of his heel before planting his foot. "You're the one that made the choice here, mister," he said to Clint. "And it was a piss-poor one." As he reached the edge of the trees, he added, "It might just cost you yer life."

With that, Sam stepped back into the shadows provided by the encroaching woods and disappeared.

Clint stepped into the clearing and looked down at Arthur.

"Thank the Lord you showed up," Arthur said in a rush. "You don't know how glad I am to see you."

"I've got a pretty good idea," Clint replied.

Reaching out with a shaky hand, Arthur said, "My name's Ar—"

"No offense," Clint interrupted. "But you might want to save the introductions for later. There was a good amount of riflemen out there and I sure as hell didn't kill them all."

While he'd been practically overjoyed a moment ago, Arthur's face once again dropped. The color drained out of him and he started nervously looking around the edges of his camp. "You think they're not really gone?"

Clint had to look at him just to make sure the fellow was serious. The look of terror on Arthur's face was plain enough to see, however, so Clint merely replied, "No. I don't think they're really gone."

"So we're not out of the woods just yet."

When Arthur said that, he glanced around at the trees surrounding them before looking to Clint with a weary smile. He tried to let out a chuckle, but Clint's somewhat confused, icy stare nipped it in the bud.

"Do you have a horse around here?" Clint asked.

Dropping his trembling smirk, Arthur nodded. "Yes. She's tethered right over—"

"I see her. You gather up your things and I'll get your horse. We should be able to make it out of here with our skins, but only if we be quick about it. There could be a whole lot more men out there."

"Of course," Arthur said as he started picking up his coffeepot and cups.

"And just take the things you absolutely need. We don't have time to clean up properly."

Freezing for a moment, Arthur let his arms drop and allowed the things he'd gathered so far clatter to the ground. Clint stared mournfully at the black coffee that was soaking into the dirt.

FIVE

Clint's shoulders were up around his ears until both he and the spindly fellow at the campsite were both well away from those woods. Every step of the way until now, Clint had been just waiting for the next ambush to be sprung or the next shot to be fired at them. However, the only rifleman they found along the way had been the dead one still laying where Clint had dropped him.

There was no trace of the other man who'd stared Clint down at the campsite. Even though the meeting had turned out fairly well from Clint's standpoint, that didn't mean that he was looking forward to another one.

When it came to the slender man now riding at Clint's side, it seemed that both men were out for a leisurely ride through the mountains. He had yet to stop talking about nothing at all. Just when he stopped to take a breath, he started up all over again.

"By the way, the name's Arthur Books," the spindly man said while extending a hand toward Clint.

Now that there was some distance between them and the spot where they'd met up, the horses were moving at an easy pace. Clint kept it that way so he could get a better look at what was going on around him while any important sounds weren't lost amid the thunder of hooves. Looking over at the hand that was stuck out in his direction, Clint had to take one more look at the fellow extending it.

Still unable to decide if Arthur was fearless, stupid, or just had a real short memory, Clint shook the man's hand. It seemed easier to just go along and not make things tougher than they already were.

Of course, his chances for an easy ride were cut down considerably when he took it upon himself to keep Arthur alive.

"And you are?"

"Clint Adams."

Arthur nodded, smiled, and looked around at the scenery. "I thought I was a dead man, that's for certain. You don't know how happy I am that you . . ." He stopped himself by snapping his fingers before saying, "That's right. You do know how happy I am."

Clint had to smile at the fellow. "For a man who almost died not too long ago, you sure talk a lot."

"Just nervous energy, I guess. Come to think of it, I have been told that very thing by some others I know. Maybe it's a character flaw."

Hearing the other man say what had drifted through his own mind made Clint feel a little bad. After all, Arthur hadn't exactly done anything wrong. At least, not so far as Clint knew.

"I wouldn't go so far as to say it's a flaw, Arthur. Just a little strange under the circumstances."

"Then perhaps I'm just a little new to this. I don't usually get held at gunpoint and rescued at the last moment like that. I don't really know how to act." Turning away from Clint, he said, "My apologies if I said anything wrong."

"No need for that. I guess I'm still a bit wound up myself." Saying that, Clint reached over to offer his own hand. "Let's start this over properly. I'm Clint Adams. Pleased to meet you."

Arthur looked down at Clint's hand. He accepted it graciously and smiled so brightly that it practically cast shadows of its own. After releasing Clint's hand, he sat up in his saddle a little straighter.

Clint let out a breath, grateful that Arthur had been put sufficiently at ease so the string of chatter that had been coming from his mouth finally came to a stop.

The break lasted for all of two seconds.

"You think they're still in there?" Arthur asked.

Taking a look to see what Arthur was talking about, he found the spindly man twisting around in his saddle to stare back at the trees they'd left behind. With the small amount of distance they'd gained, the woods looked like nothing more than a messy outcropping of timber and autumnal hues.

Clint watched the trees for a while as Eclipse slowly put them farther and farther behind them. Before too long, Clint turned and shook his head. "I wouldn't be too worried about them for a while."

Arthur nodded approvingly before snapping his head around and asking, "For a while? What do you mean?"

"I think we should have a clear shot into Mondale."

"You think?"

"Look, Arthur," Clint said, doing his best to choke back the frustration that was welling up in his gut. "Mondale is the closest town I know. We should be able to reach it without riding through too much of the night and we should make it there in one piece. That's what I mean."

While he wasn't arguing at the moment, Arthur kept shooting glances over his shoulder and fretting in his saddle. He pulled in a series of breaths and let every last one of them out in a disgruntled huff.

Finally, Clint slapped his hand on his knee and turned to look over at the horse beside him. "What is it?"

"Hmm?"

"You're squirming like you've got a tick in your britches."

"Well, I don't mean to be contrary . . ."

"Yeah. But?"

Clearing his throat, Arthur lowered his head and looked at Clint like he expected to be slapped down at any second. "But Mondale isn't the closest town from here."

"All right. Name one that's closer."

"Scorpion's Tail."

"What? I've never heard of it."

"That's no surprise. Actually, it's a small place founded by a bunch of miners who rode in from the Nevada desert after making a big enough strike to—"

"You sold me," Clint interrupted. "How far is it?"

"I'd say we can make it just after dusk. That is, if we head a little more to the northwest."

Clint had already tugged Eclipse's reins and didn't stop until Arthur nodded approvingly. "How's that?" Clint asked.

"Fine," Arthur replied. "Just fine."

Sighing, Clint shook his head and watched as the sun worked its way down behind the rocky slopes that jutted out like a hulking, bony spine in the ground. "Scorpion's Tail, huh? Sounds real friendly."

SIX

To say that Scorpion's Tail was a small place was an understatement. In fact, as he and Arthur rode into the town, Clint figured that calling the place a town might have been an understatement as well. Scorpion's Tail was wedged in the crags of a set of ridges leading up to the base of the mountains. The stretch of mountains wasn't much to behold, but it was big enough to hold up the rickety structures and fence posts that seemed to pass for civilization in Arthur's mind.

Clint might have passed it by if he was on his own. If it had been just a bit darker, he would have easily missed the nailed-together planks marking the leaning structures as a town rather than some kind of large, poorly maintained private spread. There was no way to miss the one piece of town that wasn't an eyesore. On top of what had to have been a chapel, there was a tall, slender cross that appeared to be made from silver.

The cross was dented and crooked, but it still appeared to be looking over the town like a weary guardian.

"I think I'll just ride a bit more and camp," Clint said. "You should do just fine from here."

Arthur reached over and almost grabbed hold of

Eclipse's bridle. "No, no. Don't leave just yet." He pulled his hand back and shrugged apologetically. "What I mean is that I've been here before and I know there's an excellent saloon just over there."

Clint looked over to where Arthur was pointing and saw that there was indeed a saloon. It seemed the place might fall in on itself before too long, but he figured he should be safe in there for an hour or two.

"What about a hotel?" Clint asked.

"Of course. At least, I'm pretty sure there's one here. Anyway, I'd really appreciate it if you'd stay. Buying you a drink or two is the least I can do to repay you for saving my life."

As if to add even more to Arthur's case, the sun dipped down a bit further below the horizon. The chill in the air dropped a bit more with every moment that the daylight faded away. There were plenty of places to camp, but it would be a while before Clint found one and set up well enough to get to sleep.

"I guess it would be nice to sleep on a bed tonight," Clint admitted.

Arthur reached over and patted him on the shoulder. "That's the spirit. A good night's sleep after a hot meal will make you more than happy to spend a night in Scorpion's Tail."

"Are you certain you've only been here once or twice?"

"Well, maybe more than that, but who keeps track? Anyway, the saloon is right over there."

The path leading into town wasn't so much a road as it was a wider version of a mountain trail. It led up into the outcropping and, as far as Clint could tell, all the way up to the buildings on top. Having already shed their leaves, the trees at the edge of town weren't much more than wooden skeletons. To be fair, that description fit the entire town pretty well.

Even so, Arthur rode into Scorpion's Tail like a king returning to his castle. For the most part, his joy seemed to come more from being alive at all rather than what town he was in. Clint couldn't blame him for that. By the time they climbed down from their saddles and tied up their horses outside of the saloon, Clint was feeling a lot better himself.

"Here we are," Arthur said. "Nice, isn't it?"

Clint glanced up at the place. The only thing separating this leaning wreck of a building from all the others around it was the shot-up sign hanging outside which simply read SALOON.

"Sure," Clint replied, keeping his comments to himself. "It looks great."

"You smell that? I'd say that's either meat loaf or shepherd's pie."

Before Clint could ask how the hell Arthur could tell so much, he caught a whiff for himself. Sure enough, the scents of cooked beef, potatoes, and bread wafted through the air, bringing a reflexive smile to his face.

"Come on, friend," Arthur said. "Let's get something to eat."

The saloon had more holes in it than a sieve. Even before Clint got anywhere close to the front door, he could hear everything from voices and glasses clinking together to a banjo being strummed inside. Of course, the closer he got, the more he could smell the food being cooked. If there was one thing that could redeem almost any place in Clint's mind, it was good food. So far, Scorpion's Tail was showing him a glimmer of promise.

Arthur pushed the door open and walked inside. Clint followed right behind him, taking a moment to get a look for himself before entering.

The saloon was about the size of a modest house. It was wider than it was deep and nearly every inch was cluttered with people or some sort of furniture. Not much observation was required to discover that there was only one room.

The food he'd been smelling was being prepared at a pot-belly stove in the far corner.

"Evenin', Artie," a short redhead said as she walked by. "Back so soon?"

Looking over to Clint, Arthur puffed out his chest. "People are friendly in this town, despite its name."

Clint made a sweeping forward motion with one arm and bowed slightly at the waist. "Since you're the known man, I'll let you lead the way."

"Certainly."

Arthur had no problem at all in strutting in front of Clint. He made a straight line for the closest table that wasn't occupied. It was a square surface barely wide enough for two men to place their hands flat upon its top. Still, it was plenty big enough to hold the two glasses that were set down upon it.

The woman who'd brought the drinks wasn't the same one that Clint had seen serving them moments ago. This one was Arthur's height, had a trim body and light blond hair that came down just past her shoulders. Even as Arthur's hand brushed over her hip, she had yet to take her eyes off of Clint.

"Good to see you so soon, Arthur," she said. "Who's your friend?"

Nodding in Clint's direction, Arthur replied, "His name's Clint Adams. Clint, this is Tricia Packard."

Tricia extended a hand, which Clint immediately took and kissed. That brought a warm smile to her face. "Clint Adams?" she asked while wriggling tactfully out of Arthur's grasp. "I think I've heard of you."

"Nothing bad, I hope."

Allowing her smile to turn a bit mischievous, she said, "Well, that wouldn't be much fun."

Clint nodded, feeling the heat from her eyes take away all the chill that had soaked into him throughout the cold ride. "I agree."

Having just finished his drink, Arthur looked at Clint and Tricia and reached over to slap Clint on the shoulder. "See? I told you you'd like it here."

"So, are you a friend of Arthur's?" Tricia asked.

"We ran into some trouble a ways out of town," Clint replied. "I figured I'd take his word that this was a place worth visiting."

Tricia had already positioned herself so that she was in between both men, but facing more toward Clint. Between the table and her own body, she knew she was blocking all but Clint's head and shoulders from Arthur's view. Of course, it was hard to say whether or not that would have stopped her from reaching out and sliding her hand along Clint's inner thigh.

Clint's eyes widened in pleasant surprise, and when he caught a glimpse of Arthur, the smaller man lifted his glass and nodded.

"So what do you think so far, Clint?" Tricia asked. "Are you glad you came?"

Nodding, Clint said, "And I'm getting more glad with every second."

SEVEN

The unnamed saloon turned out to be one of the best Clint had been to in a while. To be fair, he'd been sleeping on the ground more often than not for about a month, but he didn't have any reason to complain about the place so far. His only complaint was that Arthur insisted on buying whiskey for him even though Clint never even touched the first one that had been set in front of him.

As she'd done for the last hour, Tricia slinked up to Clint's side so she could replace his liquor with a beer. "You'd think he would have learned by now, wouldn't you?" she said with a shake of her head.

Arthur didn't take notice of her comment, since he was too busy trying to grope the short redhead that he'd spotted on his way into the place. The waitress would smile and bat her eyes at the right moments, but didn't get too close to the table unless it was absolutely necessary.

Although Tricia was making her own rounds throughout the saloon, she stepped up close enough for Clint to smell the smoky fragrance of her hair whenever possible. "So," she said softly into Clint's ear, "how long have you known Arthur?"

"Less than a day. Actually, I was starting to think that meeting him has been more trouble than it was worth."

Tricia smiled knowingly. "You're not the only one I've heard say that. Still, he's not a bad man and he might be headed somewhere."

Clint nodded and took in what she was saying. There had been something nagging him in the back of his head ever since he first met up with Arthur. The smaller man hadn't done anything outright suspicious, but there were plenty of unanswered questions surrounding him.

More than once, Clint had regretted chasing after the answers to questions like that. Still, he knew he would regret it even more if he just sat back and let them all go. What clinched it for him was the fact that Tricia didn't seem to mind giving up some information about Arthur.

Just as he was going to ask her a question to feel out her position regarding Arthur and what business he was truly in, Clint felt her doing some feeling of her own. Tricia's hand found its familiar spot on his thigh. This time, however, it snuck up a little farther before wandering back down again.

"This place is kind of noisy," Clint said. "Is there anywhere else we can go to talk?"

Tricia's hand immediately went to Clint's and she all but pulled him away from the table. "I thought you were never going to ask."

Until now, Arthur had been wrapped up in his own pursuits of the redhead as well as a few other women who got in his range. While he'd been leaving Clint to his own devices so far, he noticed when Clint was dragged away by Tricia.

The blonde tossed a quick glance toward Arthur and said, "I'm just going to show him around for a bit."

"But we still need to get our food," Arthur said.

"Don't worry," she replied, already turning her back on

the smaller man. "I'm sure he'll still have a plenty big appetite when he gets back."

Clint allowed himself to be pulled along by Tricia. Along the way, he looked over to Arthur and shrugged. Suddenly, Clint raised his eyebrows and pointed to the redhead who was making her way back to the table.

The redhead got a look on her face similar to a deer that had suddenly stumbled into a hunter's trap. After a quick glare at Clint and Tricia, she plastered a smile onto her face and stepped into the inescapable groping hands of Arthur Books.

"She'll be fine," Tricia said. "Arthur's been trying to get his hands under that dress of hers for so long that she probably doesn't have a stitch of clothes without his mark on it."

"Where are we going?" Clint asked. So far, he'd been led through the room and toward the stove in the back. They'd gotten plenty of looks from workers and customers alike, but nobody had gotten in their way.

"What's the matter?" she asked while turning on the balls of her feet without breaking stride. "You think I'll steal you away?"

Clint tightened his grip on her hand and pulled her toward him. Although Tricia seemed a little surprised, she wasn't about to stop him. They were at the very back of the saloon and so close to the stove that the heat from it washed over that side of their bodies.

He turned slightly and pushed Tricia up against a wall. She landed there, adding a little force on her own. Her eyes had become hungrier and it was an obvious strain for her to keep from pressing against him even harder.

Leaning forward, Clint moved in so his face was close enough for him to brush his lips against her neck. His hands wandered over her hips, which were covered with a soft, dark-brown cotton skirt. The slower his hands moved, the more her chest heaved beneath the laced front of her dark yellow blouse.

"Maybe you're the one that should be worried about being stolen away," he said. "I've been thinking about that very thing from the moment I saw you."

Tricia let out the breath she'd been holding and shifted her hips so she could brush gently against Clint's groin. "If you didn't talk so much, we'd have been out of here already."

Smiling, Clint allowed Tricia to slip past him and head for a narrow side door next to the stove. That left him there for a moment, staring into the face of a cook with a potbelly of his own and a face smeared with smoke and grease. At first, it looked as though the cook was going to say something. Then, he merely shrugged and got back to the food he was preparing.

Clint stepped through the door and found himself outside the saloon altogether. It took him a moment to find Tricia, but she was waiting for him, leaning against the doorway of a nearby smokehouse. The little shack was up against the stony ridge that made up the town's northern border.

Once she knew she'd been spotted, Tricia turned and walked into the smokehouse. One of her hands wandered up to unlace the front of her blouse, allowing that shoulder to drop down and expose smooth, bare skin.

Even before Tricia had walked into the shadows, Clint was walking in and pulling the door shut behind him.

EIGHT

The inside of the smokehouse was mostly dark, but with some of the fading sunlight able to make it through the spaces between the boards. In the space of several seconds, that sunlight disappeared altogether as the sun dipped down far enough to color the sky a dark purple. At first, when Clint stepped into the shack, he couldn't see much more than a few bulky shapes and the constant swirl of dust through the air.

Tricia moved between those shapes, which were mostly thick pieces of canvas hanging from empty hooks. Once his eyes adjusted to the growing darkness, Clint could see the dim streams of light piercing the shadows. Most of that light came from the lantern outside the saloon.

Clint stepped cautiously into the smokehouse. He glanced around until he was certain that he and Tricia were the only living things inside those rickety walls. In fact, once he was sure of that, he felt even more at ease since he could hear practically every turn of the wind outside.

Tricia had backed against the far wall. Her arms were outstretched and her blouse was open to hang off of one shoulder. The sides of her breasts peeked out from the open front of her blouse, with one of the thin streams of light spilling over them. One small, dark nipple was exposed, and grew harder as Clint walked closer.

The air smelled smoky, but it was apparent that the shack hadn't been used for its original purpose for some time. Clint walked past the hooks, pushing aside the canvas as it drifted in his way. When he got to where Tricia waited for him, he reached out to slip his hands inside the open front of her blouse.

Her skin was soft and warm to the touch. As he pushed aside the material, he could feel her tensing in anticipation while pulling in a long breath. Her slender body writhed against him. Clint moved his hands up over her body once her blouse was off, easing her arms up until they were stretching over her head.

Grasping her wrists with one hand, Clint let his other hand roam freely over her bare breasts. As much as she squirmed and softly groaned, not once did Tricia try to get her hands free from Clint's grip. On the contrary, she'd become even more excited now that she was all but trapped between him and the wall.

Clint cupped her in one hand. Tricia's breast was just enough to fit with just a little room to spare. He brushed his palm lightly against her nipple until the dark, sensitive skin became fully erect and Tricia started moaning a little louder.

Tricia's leg started sliding up and down along Clint's as she began grinding her hips against him as well. She arched her back, silently begging him to keep massaging her breast. When Clint leaned down to start kissing a line down her neck, she pulled one hand out of his grasp to run through his hair.

Her skin tasted sweet as Clint flicked his tongue gently along the base of her neck. Every so often, he would nip playfully at her skin. All the while, he kept working his way down until his lips were grazing the smooth texture between her breasts.

Tricia's fingers snaked through Clint's hair, sending his hat to the ground. Those same fingers clasped him with renewed intensity as his mouth found her nipple and his tongue made quick circles around the dark skin.

Chills worked their way under her skin that were so powerful, Clint could practically feel them for himself. His hands were moving over her body, pushing aside whatever clothing he could find before moving on to another unexplored part.

Soon, his fingers brushed against the waistband of her skirt. With a few tugs, he had the skirt down past her hips until it dropped to the floor around her ankles. When he looked back up at her, Clint found a hungry look in Tricia's eyes. Both her hands were free by now and she used them to all but tear Clint's jeans off of his body.

In no time at all, she had her hands between Clint's legs and was stroking his rigid cock in long, yearning motions. She never took her eyes away from his face, watching every shift of Clint's expression as she worked him to a powerful erection.

When Clint took a breath, he wanted nothing more than to feel Tricia's legs wrapped around him. He didn't have to say a word to let her know that. All he had to do was reach down with both hands and cup her tight little buttocks.

Tricia gave a little hop and wrapped her legs around him. By the time her ankles were locked at the small of his back, Clint had her pressed against the wall. This time, Clint was the one entangled in her grasp. And there was no other place he would rather be since Tricia quickly reached down to guide his cock between her legs.

They both held their breath for a moment and didn't let it out until Clint's rigid column of flesh was buried deep inside of her. Tricia enveloped him completely, spreading her legs just a little more so Clint could drive as far into her as he could.

He stayed where he was for a moment, savoring the feel

of their naked flesh pressed against each other as well as the powerful grip of Tricia's legs around his waist. Clint squeezed her buttocks in his hands, massaging the smooth flesh while holding her up so he could start pumping in and out of her.

Tricia's hands brushed up and down along Clint's chest before finally settling on his shoulders. She rested her head against the wall and let a little, satisfied smile ease onto her face as she felt Clint moving in her.

After a few slow strokes, Clint tightened his grip on her and started pounding with a little more force. He felt Tricia's fingers dig into his shoulders and saw her bite down on her lower lip. The most telling signal she gave was the way she pulled him in even more with her ankles every time he thrust forward.

Soon, Clint's thrusts were so strong that the wall behind Tricia started to creak against the strain. When he paused for a moment to catch his breath, Clint felt Tricia's hips pump against him with just as much force as he'd been giving to her.

"Clint," she moaned. "Don't you dare stop."

NINE

Clint was buckling his gun belt around his waist, and was just about to pick up his hat when he noticed that Tricia was watching him intently. In fact, she'd been watching him like a hawk from the moment her climax had faded to a warm tingle underneath her skin.

She still leaned against the wall. This time, however, it seemed that was the only way for her to remain on her feet. The light had faded away until all that remained was the faint glimmer being cast off of a lantern hanging outside. That little bit of light played off the front of her body as well as the blouse, which she'd pulled back on without bothering to lace it up again.

Clint had his hat in his hand, but stopped short of putting it on. Instead, he reached out and dropped the hat onto Tricia's head. She took a step forward and adjusted it so the hat sat tilted up at an angle.

"You look good in that," Clint said. "Then again, you'd look even better if that was all you had on."

"Maybe later."

"So I didn't wear out my welcome?"

"Not hardly."

"I suppose being a friend of Arthur's helped smooth things over for me, huh?"

Tricia made a show of thinking that over, but wasn't even close to being convincing. "Nah, you had the winning hand when you got here. Arthur's problem is that he's nothing but hands and they're always reaching out at the wrong time."

"Yeah, I noticed that. I wonder how many times that redhead's slapped him by now."

"Not one," Tricia said. "He's a good tipper."

"How long have you known him?" Clint asked.

"Not long. Just a month or two."

"By the sound of it, I'd say that nobody much expected him to be back in town for a while."

"He's been talking about some big trip he had planned. Supposedly, he meant to come back a rich man. Instead, he just comes back early. That's Arthur for you. He likes the sound of his own voice more than anything else, I think."

Clint took in every word Tricia said while carefully measuring out the ones he meant to say. Although he was getting some good information to work with, he knew he could bring the conversation to a stop real quickly if he pushed too hard. "He seems like a good enough sort. He did mention something about losing something that was pretty important. Since he did his part to bring us both back alive, I'd like to find it for him. You know what he might be talking about?"

Tricia's brow furrowed and she looked at Clint for a few silent moments. Although Clint knew his face wasn't giving anything away, he worried that he might have just tipped his hand. The truth of the matter was that he'd heard the gunman back at the campsite talk about something being given to Arthur that was important enough to kill for. Since Arthur liked to talk so much, Clint hoped he might have said something useful the last time he was at this saloon.

Judging by the blank look in Tricia's eyes and the way she started to shake her head, she either didn't know anything or didn't want to share it with him.

"He was waiting for something to come in on the last few stages," she said. "But I don't know what it was. The only reason I know that is because the stage drops off its deliveries to the saloon so the driver can get straight to drinking."

"I hope I'm not keeping you from anything," Clint said before she got any more suspicious. "Do you work at the saloon?"

"I run a poker game every other night and the owner likes to keep me around as much as he can. He says I'm good luck."

Clint reached out and took hold of her by the hips. Pulling her closer to him, he planted a healthy kiss on her lips. Tricia responded by opening her mouth and allowing her tongue to slide out and tease Clint's.

After catching his breath once again, Clint said, "So far, I'd have to agree."

Tricia melted into Clint's arms. Just before they could get too close to what they'd been doing a few minutes ago, Clint's eyes were drawn away from the creamy skin of her shoulder and neck. The stream of dim light coming into the smokehouse through one of the gaps in the wall had been broken by someone moving through it on their way to the door. If not for that, Clint might not have even known anyone else was out there.

"Are you expecting anyone?" Clint whispered.

Tricia shook her head. When she started to say something, she was stopped by Clint's hand over her mouth. When she saw Clint's hand moving toward his gun, she retreated into the corner where he pointed and didn't make a sound.

TEN

Whenever possible, Clint preferred to avoid sneaking around. It certainly had its advantages every now and then, but it also had one distinct disadvantage. If a man got caught sneaking around, it was a fair assumption that he was up to no good. This cut down on a lot of things like explaining yourself and bargaining.

Then again, Clint didn't mind so much when he caught other men trying to sneak up on him. His reasons for that were exactly the same as the reasons he didn't like sneaking around himself. In this case, he didn't mind doing a bit of sneaking of his own as he crept up to the door. And Clint didn't feel one bit of guilt in waiting for just the right moment before pushing that door open with a powerful burst of speed and strength.

The door flew open, but only for a foot or so before it smashed into the face of the man who'd tried to get the drop on Clint. He was a shorter fellow with dark, scraggly hair hanging down from beneath a dented bowler hat.

The shorter man reeled back as blood drizzled from his nose. A gun was already in his hand, but had been forgotten for the moment due to the disorienting pain that now washed through him.

"What're you doing here?" Clint snarled. His own hand stayed close to his Colt, but hadn't drawn the weapon just yet.

The other man grabbed for his nose with his free hand as he squinted in Clint's direction. "Yer the one that should answer that," came the man's muffled voice through his own hand.

"I'm here on my own business," Clint replied. "What about you?"

"You . . . you broke my nose!"

"Sorry about that. I was on my way out. Let me buy you a drink to make it up to you."

Now that he'd pulled himself together a little bit, the man straightened up and started to lift his gun. He noticed the Colt at Clint's side and stopped himself before taking aim. "Tell me whatever you heard from Books and we'll call it even."

"Arthur?"

"Yeah. Arthur Books. An' don't bother sayin' you don't know him because I know better. You pulled his fat from the fire an' killed one of my friends in the process."

"Does this friend of yours have a fondness for rifles and hiding out in the woods?"

The man's eye twitched and his hand clenched around his gun. "Yeah. That's the one."

"Then you should probably know that your friend tried to gun me down." Clint paused and studied the fellow's face as though he was sitting across from him at a poker table. "But I'm sure you already knew that. Were you one of the other ones there? One of the ones I let get out of those woods with their life?"

Although the other man didn't answer that question directly, the look on his face and the shifting of his eyes told Clint all he needed to know.

"What'd Books tell you?" the man asked. "It can't mean nothing to you and it'll end this little conversation nice and easy."

"Sounds good to me. Let's see, he told me all about his fondness for whiskey, the history of Scorpion's Tail, some bad jokes. Oh, and I did ask him how he brewed his coffee. Is that what you're after?"

Now, the man did aim his gun a bit more in Clint's direction. "Cut the bullshit. You know what I'm after."

"Afraid I don't."

"Yeah? Well, that's too bad." Shifting his eyes toward the smokehouse, he asked, "Who you got in there? That sweet little redhead from the saloon?"

"Nope."

"Whoever she is, I reckon it's my turn with her now."

"You can still go the nice and easy route, you know. Just drop that pistol and be on your way."

The confident smirk on the man's face was starting to fade. It wasn't so much because of what Clint was doing. It was more due to what he wasn't doing. So far, Clint had yet to move from his spot or even show the slightest bit of wavering in his voice. Clint's eyes hadn't even looked away from the man's face.

The more he thought about those things, the tenser the man got.

Clint could read that much without having to try. The anticipation hung in the air like an approaching lightning storm, sending crackles underneath both men's skin.

The man with the broken nose sniffed up a bit of blood, feeling a jolt of pain that must have been enough to push him right over the edge. His grip tightened around his pistol and he pivoted at the elbow to bring the weapon up.

In the time it took for the man's arm to bend, Clint had snatched his Colt from its holster, taken aim, and fired. He did so in a blur of motion, punctuated with a single shot that cracked through the air like a whip.

The man's bloodied face was illuminated by sparks for half a second, freezing the expression that he would take with him to the grave. His head lolled forward, allowing blood from his nose to drip onto his boots. Blood was now dripping from the hole in his chest to be soaked up by his clothes to form a black stain.

His knees buckled and he dropped back, hitting the ground with a solid thump.

The barrel of Clint's Colt followed the man all the way down. Smoke curled up from it until it was finally lowered back into its holster. Clint kept his eye on the man for a few more seconds before stepping forward and kicking the gun away from the corpse's hand.

When he heard the door rattle behind him, Clint reflexively spun on the balls of his feet. Although he didn't draw the Colt, his hand had dropped in that direction.

Tricia hopped away from the door with a start.

"It's all right," Clint said, offering her his hand. "You can come out of there."

"Is he . . . ?"

"Yeah," Clint replied. "But don't worry about him. I've got a job for you. Think you're up to it?"

"As long as you don't mind me shaking like a leaf."

ELEVEN

Arthur sat at his spot with a plate of food in front of him. Actually, Clint's food had arrived not too long ago but neither one of the plates had been touched. Even though the scent of the meat and bread had been drifting through Arthur's nostrils for a few minutes, he'd somehow lost his appetite.

The most obvious reason for that was the armed killer who'd taken the seat across from him and was looking at him with death in his eyes.

"What's the matter, Artie?" the killer asked. "Didn't you miss me?"

It took a few moments for Arthur to pull enough air into his lungs to form a word, but he sputtered that out in a few random syllables. He did fare a little better on his second try, however.

"Actually," Arthur said, "I thought you would've gone your own way by now, Sam."

The armed man didn't look much different than when he'd been holding Arthur at gunpoint at his campsite not too long ago. He was a bit dustier and definitely madder, but other than that pretty much the same. "You didn't think

I'd be scared away that easily, did you? I still want to know what he sent you."

Arthur nudged his fork and looked down at his plate like a kid staring at an unwanted helping of greens.

Drawing his gun, Sam slammed the pistol onto the table and kept his hand on top of it. Although most of the others in the saloon had been minding their business up to now, the sound of iron pounding against the table was enough to draw some attention. Sam didn't seem to mind.

"I'm tired and I want to get some sleep," Sam grunted. "I'm hungry and there's plenty other things I'd rather be doing than talking to you about the same goddamn thing. So you either talk right now or you'll be eating lead instead of that supper you ordered."

Arthur's eyes darted around the room and his mouth trembled.

"Who're you lookin' for?" Sam asked. "If it's that asshole who bailed you out the last time, I wouldn't bother."

Just then, the door near the stove flapped open and Tricia stumbled inside. She was white as a ghost and staggered as though she was about to pass out. "He's dead," she said to the man behind the bar. "Clint's dead. He was gunned down out by the smokehouse."

"That fella you were with?" the barkeep asked.

Tricia nodded. "He's dead."

Both Arthur and Sam had been watching her. By the time someone came to comfort Tricia, Arthur was even paler than she was. Sam, on the other hand, looked like the cat that swallowed the canary.

"See?" Sam asked. "You got no more backup and you sure as hell don't have anyone in this town who likes you enough to die for you. Hand over whatever it is you're hiding or I'll kill you and take it myself. Either way, you won't be seeing a penny of that money."

Sucking in a deep breath, Arthur pushed away from the

table and stood in front of Sam. He knocked his chair over to the floor behind him, which brought a sudden silence to the room.

"If that's the way you want it," Arthur said. "Then so be it. At least I'll go down fighting."

Sam watched Arthur as if he couldn't quite believe what he was seeing. When Arthur pulled open his jacket to show the gun handle jutting out from under his belt, Sam actually started to laugh.

"That's downright sweet," Sam said mockingly. "You surprised me, Arthur. At least you're good for that much."

"Actually," came a voice from behind Sam, "you surprised me too."

Without letting Arthur completely out of his sight, Sam shifted in his seat so he could get a look at who'd just spoken. He saw enough of the figure sidling up to him to confirm his suspicions. "I didn't see you sneak in here, Adams."

"I know. Too bad the man you sent out after me wasn't as good at distraction. If he was, maybe he'd still be alive right now."

"I heard you were dead," Arthur said in disbelief.

"I must admit," Clint said as he took his position at the table, "I started that rumor myself. At least that bought me the time I needed to walk in through the front door. Imagine my surprise when I saw you here," he said to Sam. "I thought I told you to make yourself scarce."

"So it's really Clint Adams, huh?" Sam asked. "I heard you were in the area and one of my men said he recognized your face, but I didn't think it could be you. What would The Gunsmith want with this little turd?"

Arthur straightened up in response to that comment. Despite the fact that his hand was even closer to the gun stuck in his belt, nobody really seemed to pay him any mind.

"Come on, Arthur," Clint said. "This one's a whole lot

of talk and not much else. I prefer to eat my food without so many distractions."

When he saw Clint step away from the table and start walking toward the door, Arthur didn't quite know what to do. He took a few tentative steps toward the door as well, but still kept his hand near his gun. Once he saw that Sam might actually let him go, Arthur practically bolted to Clint's side.

Sam watched the two men, and didn't make a move until Clint was already stepping out the door. When Sam turned around, he swept his arm over the table and sent both plates as well as all the food upon them flying through the air.

"You chicken shit!" he yelled. "Don't you just turn your back on me, Adams! Come back here, goddammit!"

Clint stepped outside and kept walking. Arthur had taken up the spot beside him and was yapping about something or other, but Clint was too busy to listen to that. His ears were only attuned to a specific set of sounds. One of them was the sound of Sam's raging voice. The other was the sound of heavy footsteps clomping over the boards in front of the saloon.

He only had to wait a few seconds before hearing both of those sounds in quick succession.

"Nobody puts their back to Sam Marker! Nobody, you hear! I'll get what I came for and I'll get it right now!"

"I never knew what you were talking about," Clint said over his shoulder. "And I still don't."

"Bullshit. Not that it makes any difference."

At that moment, Clint heard something else he'd been waiting for. It was a subtle shift in Sam's voice that was like a dog growling in the back of its throat rather than whining for food.

Clint turned around and faced Sam. There wasn't anything left for him to say, so he didn't bother speaking. The fact that one gunman had already been sent for him was more than enough to let Clint know what Sam's intentions were. The fact that a gun was still gripped in Sam's hand at the moment only drove that point home like a nail in a coffin.

The look on Sam's face was a mix of cocky arrogance and grim satisfaction. He'd finally gotten Clint to stop and listen. He was also about to take the gamble that so many other would-be gunfighters only dreamed of.

Clint stood his ground without making a move. It wasn't his way to back down, but he was never one to pick a fight.

The fight came to him when Sam's hand clenched around his pistol and brought the gun up in a quick snap. His finger was squeezing the trigger as he was taking aim, but Clint's hand had already snapped into motion as well.

In one fluid movement, Clint drew the modified Colt and took his shot.

The bullet caught Sam through one eye, lifting him up like a solid punch under the jaw before dropping him dead onto the boards.

Clint walked forward and dropped the Colt back into its holster. He stepped over Sam and headed back into the saloon.

"Where are you going?" Arthur asked. "What if there's more of them?"

"They can find me in here. I'm still hungry."

TWELVE

Scorpion's Tail lived up to its deadly-sounding name in more ways than one. Not only had Clint had to gun down two men since his arrival, but those two bodies didn't seem like an unusual sight to the people who witnessed the shooting. On the contrary, the bodies were dragged away and not much else was said about it.

Clint sat in the saloon, ordered a meal to replace the one that had been tossed onto the floor, and half-expected to be brought up on charges for the shootings. At the very least, he thought someone might come along to question him about what had happened.

The only one to ask him anything, as it turned out, was the redheaded waitress. That was only to confirm his order.

"So there's no law here?" Clint asked.

Arthur shrugged. "I've never seen any. Then again, I haven't really checked."

"Now why am I having a hard time believing that?"

"Sometimes someone tries to keep the peace, but I guess there haven't been any elected sheriffs or anything of that sort."

Clint nodded and kept his eyes firmly glued to Arthur.

"All right," Arthur said, buckling under the weight of Clint's stare. "The town's lawless and I've always known it."

"There now. Was it so hard to just come out and say something for a change?"

Actually, going by the look on Arthur's face and the paleness of his skin, it wasn't all that easy. He put on a smile, but wasn't fooling anyone into thinking that he was truly so carefree as to mean it. "I, uh, think I need a drink. Can I get you one?"

"Sure. A beer."

Arthur snapped his fingers and walked away from the table. While a few of the people had cleared out of the saloon with the gunshots, most of those had already found their way back inside. The ones that stayed away had already been replaced by a fresh batch.

The moment Arthur got to the bar, Tricia stepped up beside him.

"What happened out there?" Arthur asked.

"Hobart's dead," Tricia replied quickly. "He came after me and Clint. The rest isn't your concern."

"Did you tell him anything?"

"Not really, especially since I don't know much. If it makes you feel any better, I don't think he knows about anything that's going on between you and Kane."

"There isn't much to make me feel better at the moment," Arthur said. When a glass of whiskey was set in front of him, he added, "Except for this." He downed the whiskey in one gulp and winced as the firewater burned a path down his throat.

Tricia waved at Clint, who was watching them both from his table. "He saved my life, you know," she told Arthur.

"And mine. Twice. You don't have to remind me."

"He's got his suspicions. He'd have to be a damn fool not to have plenty of those by now. It'd save you a lot of trouble if you just brought him in on this deal of yours."

When she saw the fiery glare she got from Arthur, Tricia quickly added, "Whatever that deal may be. At least it's safe to say that whatever you've got cooking, Clint can help you survive long enough to talk about it."

The intensity in Arthur's eyes died down almost as quickly as it had flared up. "Yeah. I wasn't sure about that until now. If he could handle Sam, then he might be able to stand up to Kane. Well, at least he should have a fighting chance."

"Or Clint might not even want to bother," Tricia pointed out. "I doubt you could make him do anything he doesn't want to. Don't you think he's at least earned the right to make the decision for himself?"

"Yeah," Arthur said. "I sure do."

Tricia leaned up against him a bit more and slid her hand along Arthur's arm. "You know, I might be able to help you myself if I knew about this big secret of yours."

"You know plenty already."

Pouting seductively with her lower lip, she squeezed his arm a bit more. "Not really, I don't. I sure would like to. Maybe you'd like to tell that redhead you've had your eye on. I bet I could arrange for a meeting between just the two of you."

Although that seemed to hit Arthur a bit deeper than anything else so far, he found something deep inside to strengthen his resolve. "When this is over, I'll get her myself. Now, if you'll excuse me, I need to talk to Clint."

THIRTEEN

Clint watched Arthur and Tricia's conversation so closely that he could practically feel every twitch they made. He studied the way they looked at each other as well as the way they sometimes looked back at him. There was plenty to learn from the way someone stood or shifted on their feet and Clint could tell plenty by watching those two at the bar.

Arthur was plainly nervous, but he was always a little nervous. He was distracted by the smooth advances Tricia was putting on him, which told Clint that she was angling for something herself. If they were in on something together, then Tricia wasn't a full partner. As far as Arthur went, he was holding some of the cards, but not all of them.

That meant there was still plenty of ground to be covered. It also gave Clint a few more key pieces of information to add to all the rest.

When Arthur came back to the table, he had to stop and go back to the bar to replace the second whiskey he'd bought with a beer. He set the mug down in front of Clint with a sheepish grin, and then sat down so he could stare directly into his own glass.

"You look shaky, Arthur," Clint said in an even tone. "Is something wrong?"

Arthur looked up at Clint, started to say something, but then stopped short so he could toss back some of the whiskey. He swallowed the liquor and wiped his mouth with the back of his hand. "Nothing's wrong. Well, nothing more than those men gunning for us."

"There's more to it than that. After all, it's not like those gunmen just stumbled on us both by accident. They were after something."

Clint paused to give Arthur a chance to step in. Even though the smaller man didn't take that chance, Clint watched him carefully and read all the little things that Arthur's twitching face and darting eyes could tell him.

"All right then," Clint said. "I'll start. First of all, I know you were lying to me."

Arthur's eyes widened. "A-about what?"

"You're more well known around this town than I am, and I usually have killers calling me out on a daily basis."

"I guess that's true enough."

"You made it sound like you just passed through here once or twice."

"Yeah. Sorry about that."

"Also, I know that you had some kind of deal going on with that gunman who came after us both today."

Arthur looked more nervous than shocked about that one. "I guess you would have figured that out by now."

"I think my horse has figured that out by now."

That brought a smirk to Arthur's face. When he took another drink this time, it was more to settle his nerves rather than give him enough courage to move on.

"I didn't expect you to bare your soul to me," Clint said. "You never really asked for my help, after all. Even so, I don't like being lied to and to be honest, it seems like you could use all the help you can get. This makes two times you've almost been killed and that's just in the past day."

"I appreciate everything you've done for me, Clint. Honestly. The funny thing is that I was having a talk like this with Tricia over there."

"Does she know what's going on?"

"Not really," Arthur replied. "Part, but not the whole thing."

"Whatever you do with your business is your choice. But, in my opinion, you could sure use some good advice. I know a thing or two about staying alive when the cards are stacked against you."

Arthur nodded slightly and glanced up at Clint. This time, he was the one studying the other man's eyes. He must have seen enough to make a decision because he set his drink aside and dug for something in his pocket.

Clint watched as Arthur twisted and fidgeted in his chair. One by one, he patted down all of his pockets before finally settling on the one at his left hip. While it might have been missed by most anyone else, Clint was able to pick up on the fact that Arthur had actually taken something from the second pocket he'd checked. Checking all the others had been a show, probably meant for a distraction as to where the real item was kept.

Whatever it was that Arthur was holding, it must have been pretty important to him.

"This," Arthur said while extending a hand that was still balled into a fist, "is what Sam was after. Well, part of it anyhow."

Clint's imagination ran wild. After all the fuss, he couldn't help but anxiously lean forward and wait to see what it was Arthur was holding. Even though the man's fist didn't seem to want to come open, Clint was trying to figure out what was big enough and valuable enough to be protected within those tightly clamped fingers.

It could have been money or gold, but surely there wasn't enough in his hand to cause so much fuss. It could have been a sample from a bigger stash somewhere, which seemed fairly reasonable.

It could even be some kind of jewel. Clint had heard of some robberies where the money and gold was just a distraction to take attention away from a few diamonds that were small enough to fit in a coin purse.

All of these thoughts, plus plenty of others, raced through Clint's mind as he waited for Arthur to open his fist. Finally, Clint's anticipation grew into frustration and he looked up at Arthur's face to see if there was an end in sight.

Sensing Clint's aggravation, Arthur quickly nodded and said, "Sorry. I've kind of gotten used to keeping a close eye on this. All right then. Here it goes."

Arthur's hand opened to reveal an oddly shaped pebble.

The pebble wasn't made out of anything valuable as far as Clint could tell. It wasn't even shiny.

At that moment, all of the thoughts that had filled Clint's head were replaced by one single question.

What the hell had he been thinking when he'd chosen to ride to Colorado instead of California?

FOURTEEN

"What is it?" Clint asked.

At the moment, there wasn't one answer that Clint could think of that would make him feel any differently about what he'd just been shown.

Arthur, on the other hand, looked as though he'd just given Clint the keys to the vault and was allowing him to take whatever he could get his hands on. "It's called Christmas Rock. I probably don't have to tell you why."

Sure enough, with a slightly more careful glance, Clint could figure that one out for himself. The pebble was slightly smaller than a silver dollar. It was oval-shaped and colored with jagged, uneven stripes that were a rich green and dark red.

"It reminds me of mistletoe," Arthur said without provocation. "Or is it holly? Either way, isn't it beautiful?"

After giving Arthur another moment to make good on the previous promise, Clint sat back in his chair and said, "I'm either missing something or I'm not getting the whole story here. Is that rock valuable for some reason?"

Arthur brought the pebble in so he could take a closer look at it himself. "It's not worth much on its own. Rather, its value comes from what it leads to."

"And what's that?"

"Only a series of mines that have been lost for over fifteen years that are so full of gold and silver that they've been sought after since the moment they were discovered."

"Arthur, please tell me you've seen these mines for yourself. Because if all of this turns out to be due to some old miner's tale, then I might just lose my temper."

"Old miner's tale?"

"Every town in gold country is full of them. Even the towns within a week's ride of gold country have a few. They all sound real good, but not one of them is good for anything but a good story. And they sure as hell aren't worth spilling blood over."

Despite the pessimism in Clint's voice, Arthur was still grinning happily down at his Christmas Rock. That grin only faded a little when he glanced around suspiciously and closed his fist around the pebble. Lowering his voice so even Clint could barely hear it, he said, "This isn't just another story, Clint. It's a legend around here. It's the namesake for this whole town."

"I've never turned away from a good story. Let's hear it."

Arthur was only too happy to comply. "About fifteen years ago, there were these five miners who rode all the way out here from their homes back East. They were brothers or best friends, but they all knew enough about sniffing out gold to sell everything they owned to finance a trip into the Rockies.

"They didn't find much, but they did pull together more than most. They got at least enough to keep digging until they found that big strike. They panned in every river between the Mississippi and the Pacific Ocean, back and forth, before they found something to make it all worth their while."

"That's a lot of panning," Clint said dryly. "Let me guess. They found that Christmas Rock?"

Nodding at first, Arthur soon corrected himself and

started shaking his head. "Ye—well, no. Actually, they all found little things in this area where they were digging that struck them as peculiar. They kept them at first just as something they could send home to their families. You know, as mementos from their travels."

"Sure. Go on."

"In this particular area, they eventually found an opening to a cave that led down into these mines which were so well hidden that the only way a man could find them was by sheer, blinding, luck. The story goes that every one of these miners thought they'd died and gone to heaven. Then, when they realized that they were still on God's green earth, they figured they just had to be the most blessed men alive."

Just then, the redhead approached their table carrying yet another pair of plates heaped with food. She set them down in front of Clint and Arthur with a polite smile and a nervous glance toward Clint's holster. Between that gun and Arthur's roaming hands, she had more than enough reason to hustle away from the table and leave them to their meal.

As Clint picked up his knife and fork, he saw that Arthur was beaming at him as though he'd uncovered a brick of gold from beneath his mashed potatoes.

"I've got to be honest with you," Clint said as he cut into his meat. "I've heard some mighty tall miner's tales, and they all sound a lot like the one you just told me."

"But there's more," Arthur said. "As the miners realized just how much money they had, they loaded themselves up with as much as they could carry and headed away. Of course, they wanted to find their way back again, because there was enough left in the mines to make all of their families rich for . . . well . . . maybe forever.

"Since they'd stumbled upon the mines in the middle of a tangled knot of mountains, woods, and God only knows what else, they set up a trail of clues so they could find their way back again."

"Clues, huh?"

"That's right," Arthur said while nodding and shoveling food into his face while somehow still talking. "They each picked one clue and then headed back to the closest town. See, they were thinking that even though they themselves could find their way back again, they wanted it so their families could find their way to the mines as well. You know, to look after them."

"Real generous."

"Of course, friendships started breaking down when they realized that they weren't close to a town that suited their needs. They'd been in the mining game for long enough to know they couldn't draw attention to themselves once they found a big strike. But they still needed supplies to keep on digging.

"So what did they do?" After waiting for a moment, Arthur held out his arms as though he was motioning to the entire room.

"They built this saloon?" Clint guessed.

"No. They built this whole town."

Glancing around at the rickety walls, leaning posts, and dirty floors, Clint said, "You'd think they could afford to build a better one than this."

"All they wanted was a base camp, but they didn't want anyone else to know it was a base camp. So they founded this town and named it after one of their daughters or something."

"I feel sorry for any little girl named Scorpion's Tail."

Laughing while shaking his head, Arthur explained, "That's not the town's original name. It got that name once the miners started fighting among themselves over rights to the mines they'd discovered. You see, once the men who founded the town started getting killed, the folks who'd come here started to think there was a curse on the place.

"The killing stopped once all the original miners were dead and buried. After that, folks said that it was this town that killed them because they were too soft to live up here instead of their comfortable homes back East. Killed them just as quickly as the wrong end of a scorpion's tail."

"Has anyone else pieced all of this together?"

Reluctantly, Arthur nodded. "Yes, but they're dead too."

Clint shrugged as he cut another piece of meat and used it to scoop up some potatoes. "I guess I can see why the name for the town's stuck for so long."

FIFTEEN

"So that Christmas Rock is supposed to be one of the clues?" Clint asked.

"Not just supposed to be. It is."

"I don't suppose you have any proof of that."

Arthur got a smirk on his face that was different than the last few he'd been sporting. In fact, this one made Clint start to squirm in his seat as though he was missing something so important that it was funny. "Oh, I've got proof all right," he said before Clint could get too cautious. "And it comes from a pretty reliable source."

Arthur refused to say anything else until they'd finished their meal. For the rest of the time they were in the saloon, Arthur acted as though he was the one who'd walked through fire instead of being the one to almost die on two occasions before spilling everything he knew to Sam Marker. That confidence even grew when he allowed Clint to pay for the meal before strutting out of the saloon like he owned it.

Rather than buy into the other man's delusions, Clint merely followed Arthur and kept his eyes open. It wasn't as though he had any better plans for the evening, since Tricia had left the saloon sometime before the meal was over.

Scorpion's Tail looked even smaller and more run-down in the black of night. With only a few scattered lanterns here and there, the place looked deserted. The only signs of life came from the saloon as well as the hotel that Arthur had pointed out earlier. Other than that, there was just the occasional footstep and hushed voice to break the cold silence.

Clint truly felt the mountains around him even though he couldn't see them. There were special types of cold that were as distinct as the different kinds of heat. There was a kind of breezy, frosty cold that came in the winter on a prairie. There was a biting, bone-chilling cold that came when icy winds blew off of a lake into ten-foot-deep drifts. And then there was a mountain cold that wrapped around a man like a blanket that had been soaked in runoff from the snowy peaks.

It was that type of cold that hit Clint in the face and kept right on chipping away at him as he followed Arthur from one shadow to another. He'd pulled on some gloves and turned up the collar of his jacket, which seemed to help a bit, but Clint was still starting to shiver all the same.

"Wherever we're going," Clint grunted, "we'd best get there soon. Otherwise, I'm heading back to the hotel."

"We're already here," Arthur said, standing proudly in front of another run-down building in the midst of several other run-down buildings.

Clint looked the building up and down to see if he could spot what was so special about it. As far as he could tell, it was constructed just as poorly as all the others in town. "I'm not in the mood for guessing games, Arthur. Tell me what I'm looking at."

"Town Hall. Well, as close as you can get in Scorpion's Tail. It's where all the records are kept. Records like the town's charter."

"Looks like they're not worried about anyone running

off with it. My guess is we'll be out of some of this wind if we get inside, so let's go."

Clint led the way and Arthur was more than happy to follow. The door opened easily enough, scraping on cold, rusted hinges in a way that sounded like a cat being ripped apart in a cotton gin. Despite the grating sound, Clint was happy to step through the door as at least some of the night air was stopped by the walls around him.

The building was narrow and seemed taller than it was simply because there was no floor to separate the two levels. Instead, there appeared to be a walkway that circled the second level. Without proper lighting, Clint guessed that the walkway was just as shabby as the rest of the structure. Even with proper lighting, there was no way in hell he was about to go up there and test it for himself.

Arthur wasn't about to test his luck on the upper floor either. Instead, he walked over to the other side of the room and pointed toward the wall. As Clint drew closer, Arthur even started poking at the wall with an excited, stabbing finger.

"This is it," Arthur said. "The town's charter. Well, what passes for it anyway. Take a look for yourself."

Once he was certain that Arthur was serious, Clint stepped forward to take a look for himself. Before he could ask for it, a lantern was found, lit, and brought forward so he could get a better look at the weathered parchment tacked onto the wall by three rusty nails.

It really wasn't much of a town charter. In fact, it was more of a casual declaration from a few men who'd signed the same piece of paper that their camp was to be considered a town. By the looks of it, not a whole lot of thought had gone into the wording, but anyone who'd gotten a look at Scorpion's Tail wouldn't be too surprised by that.

After skimming through half of the scribbled words, Clint looked over to Arthur. "What am I supposed to be seeing here?"

Arthur pointed at the bottom half of the parchment. "Right there," he said excitedly. "Read that part right there."

Clint squinted and peered in closer. All the edges of the parchment were ripped or chewed away by various bugs or rodents. Although most of the words were either faded, smeared, or gone completely, there were a few that he could string together. The part Arthur wanted him to read was short and simple:

> *We'll each leave you something so you can find your way back. Just look for the silver cross and you can follow the steps from there.*

"That's an odd way to end a town charter," Clint said.

Nodding, Arthur replied. "That's because the only reason it's in the charter is so it would be posted for all to see. Also, there's no reason for anyone to steal it. Even when a few folks did figure it out, most everyone in town knew about what it said so stealing it wouldn't make much difference."

"Figure what out?"

"The clue."

Clint thought for a moment and shrugged. "Does the silver cross mean something? I think I saw a cross like that in town."

Arthur shook his head.

"You know," Clint said in a strained voice, "this would go along so much better if you just said what you needed to say rather than make me guess."

"That cross is just to throw people off the track. Here's what I as well as a few others figured out." Arthur squared his shoulders and looked directly into Clint's eyes. He spoke with more confidence and fire in his voice than Clint would have even thought possible from the spindly little man. "Each of the miners who founded this town was buried in a different spot. Since they killed each other off, they all died within a span of about eight months.

"When they died, they sent their belongings to their families. It was personal effects mostly, but each of the families got something to put them on the right path to their real inheritance."

"Speed it up, Arthur," Clint said. "It's getting awfully cold in here."

Kneeling down and reaching into his boot, Arthur said, "Each of the families got one of these."

He held out his hand and opened it just enough to allow what appeared to be a pendant to drop down and swing from a chain. Clint was about to lose a bit more of his patience until the pendant caught some of the light being cast by the lantern.

It was actually a small crucifix.

A silver crucifix.

Suddenly, Clint wasn't bothered by the cold so much anymore. Hearing Arthur's story and seeing the crucifix, some of the pieces that he'd been given were starting to fit together.

"Each member of the family got one of those?" Clint asked.

Arthur nodded.

"How'd you get it?"

"One of the miner's daughters sold it because she thought her father hadn't left her anything but a shabby house in the middle of a shabby town. She's passed on."

"And you think that's the silver cross from the charter?"

"I sure do."

"So what does that have to do with these mines you're talking about?"

"Remember what I said about the miners' graves?" Arthur asked.

"Yeah. They're scattered all around here."

"Well, this crucifix is the same as the others sent to all the miners' kin. Right down to this." Saying that, Arthur turned the crucifix around to show Clint an engraving on the back.

"Hoj?" Clint asked, reading off the crucifix.

"Not hoj. HOJ. They're initials. Specifically," Arthur said, while pointing back to the charter, "his initials."

Sure enough, Henry Obred Josefson was one of the men who'd signed the charter. Clint looked at that and then back to the crucifix. He thought it through and the longer he contemplated it, the more of an anxious look he got from Arthur.

"You said all of those crucifixes had those same initials on them?" Clint asked.

Arthur nodded.

Clint glanced back to the charter and read it through. Yet another piece fit snugly into place.

"How scattered are those graves?" Clint asked.

"As far as they can be from each other while still being about thirty paces from town. Folks say that's how the miners wanted it because they wound up hating each other so much."

"Look for the silver cross and you can find your way from there," Clint recited from the charter. "If that's the silver cross," he said, pointing to the crucifix, "and if every one of them had one man's initials on it, then that's where the trail is supposed to start."

"Yes!" Arthur said loudly enough to rattle the shack around him. "And they left enough clues to form a trail."

"That Christmas Rock is one step on the trail?"

"It sure is."

"So all you need is probably four more clues to take you to the end of the trail."

"Actually," Arthur said, "it could be 'we' who follows that trail. And," he added, "we only need three more clues."

SIXTEEN

Before too long, the temperature dropped until it was even too cold for Arthur to want to stay out in it. Although they were inside what passed for a town hall, the walls weren't solid enough to stop a strong breeze. The mountain cold seeped through the cracks like ghostly fingers to rake up and down along the two men's spines.

Arthur led Clint to a good place to put Eclipse up for the night. It seemed that the residents of Scorpion's Tail knew enough to make a sturdy stable. Not even a crazy miner would want to be stranded there without a healthy horse.

After that, he showed Clint to the hotel. Now that he was no longer trying to act like a stranger in the town, Arthur walked with his head held a little higher than before. Of course, although the folks there recognized him, they didn't seem overly happy to have him there. But Arthur was too excited to notice any of that. It was all he could do to contain himself until he could resume their conversation someplace where they wouldn't be overheard.

Clint got a good enough look at his room when he opened the door that he just tossed in his saddlebags and headed right back out again. Arthur followed him the whole time, like an overly anxious puppy who couldn't wait to fetch another bone.

Once they got to the hotel's small sitting room, they each pulled a chair close to the fireplace and warmed their hands. Rather than wait for Arthur to burst, Clint went ahead and gave the other man what he'd been waiting for.

"So," Clint said. "You really think there's something worth going after? You really think there's some mother lode waiting to be dug up?"

Arthur nodded fiercely. "Yes, I do. I thought these rumors were just stories too, until I started really finding some of these clues."

"You said you have another one?"

Glancing around the room, Arthur reached underneath his belt to retrieve a folded piece of leather that blended in seamlessly with the rest of the belt. If nothing else, Clint had to give the man credit for being awfully good at hiding things on his person.

Unfolding the leather, he showed what was inside to Clint.

"Looks like an arrowhead," Clint pointed out.

"It is."

"And how do you know it's got anything to do with this lost mine?"

"Because . . . because of where I found it."

Clint narrowed his eyes and fixed them on Arthur.

It wasn't long before the other man broke down and said, "All right, I got it off of one of the miners' bodies."

"Jesus, Arthur."

"He doesn't have any more family. Well, none that I know of anyway. It wasn't even in his pockets or anything. It was attached to the coffin. The point is that it's one of the clues. I know it."

"Let's see them," Clint said, holding out his hand.

Arthur placed the arrowhead and the Christmas Rock on Clint's palm and looked around at the few others in the hotel. So far, nobody else seemed to be taking much notice of them.

"This rock looks like it was in a river," Clint said. "I don't know a lot about the subject, but the colors look like rust or some kind of mineral. The arrowhead could be Apache. It's hard to say, though." Flipping it over, he added, "The colors are a little odd. But that could just be because it's old."

"I think these are enough to get a jump on finding those mines," Arthur said. "I've been researching this for some time now and I'm pretty sure I can find them. It might take some searching, but I can do it. The only problem is that there are other clues out there and, as far as I can tell, they've all been found."

Clint nodded while handing back the rock and arrowhead. Rubbing his hands together near the fire, he said, "I was wondering when you'd get around to that. Let me guess. This is where those gunmen come in, right?"

"More or less. I was starting to think that it was just a matter of time before they forced me to hand over my clues as well as everything I know."

"But they're dead now."

Arthur lowered his eyes and stashed his clues in his pocket. From there, he held his hands out toward the fire as well. "Sam's dead anyway. And Hobart. They were sent by a man named Jervis Kane. It might take a while before he hears that they're dead, but he'll either send someone else or come here himself once he gets that bit of news."

"Maybe you should just give this up. Seriously, Arthur, this can't be the first time you've heard stories about some buried gold or some mine that supposed to be packed full of something or other."

"No, but this is the first story I believe. I've got proof, Clint. And if I find it . . ." Arthur allowed himself to trail off for a moment before pulling in a breath and straightening up. "When I find it, it'll be worth all the trouble.

There's enough in there for everyone. There's even enough to make this a proper town. I know that it was just slapped together to cover up a base camp, but folks live here now. Folks with families. The least they deserve is a roof over their heads that keeps out the rain and some of the cold."

Clint studied Arthur carefully as he spoke. Although there was plainly desperation in the other man's words, they seemed heartfelt. Arthur might have tried to pull some wool over Clint's eyes, but considering what he thought was at stake, it seemed almost reasonable. Besides, Clint had been able to tell when Arthur was hiding something, which was just as good as knowing when the man was being completely honest. Since Arthur had started laying everything out for him, Clint hadn't been able to spot one lie in what he was saying.

There might have been plenty of stretches of the imagination, but no outright lies.

"I'd like you to come with me as I follow the trail, Clint," Arthur said. "We'd be equal partners and there's plenty to be made."

"Why would you want me to come along?" Clint asked. Even though he had a good idea of what the reason was, he wanted to see if Arthur was going to say it or try to pull some more wool.

"Because without someone to cover me, I doubt I'd make it back alive."

That was the truth as far as Clint could see it. Even so, he was more surprised by his own response. "All right, Arthur. You got yourself a partner."

SEVENTEEN

The plan was for Clint to meet up with Arthur again by the stables at dawn. After everything that had happened, Clint still didn't have any trouble falling asleep. He needed his rest and he got a few hours before he started tossing and turning.

When he awoke, the sky was still black as pitch. That gave Clint plenty of time to think over what he'd agreed to do.

He'd heard more than enough wild stories from drunk miners himself. Most of them were too wild to be believed and some of them were too wild to be a lie. The one thing they had in common was that none of those stories came with a shred of proof.

Not only did Arthur's story have some facts behind it, but some of those facts could actually be held in the palm of his hand. What got to him even more was the fact that he was starting to see something in Arthur's story besides overblown hearsay and drunken lies. Some of it actually made sense. And if there wasn't gold to be found in the mountains and streams of the West, there wouldn't have been such a rush to find it in the first place.

Realizing that trying to get any more sleep was a lost

cause, Clint rolled off of his bed and pulled on his boots. Actually, calling the slats holding up a flat sack of stuffing beneath his body a bed was stretching the term. It was only slightly better than sleeping on the ground.

As he stretched and felt the growing number of kinks in his back, neck, and shoulders, Clint had to amend that thought. It was better than sleeping on a rock.

At least, it was better than sleeping on a sharp rock.

It only took a step and a half to reach his door and once he was outside, Clint immediately caught the scent of smoke and fresh bread. His nose led him to the hotel's kitchen, where a middle-aged woman was busy stoking a fire and arranging various things on a small round table.

She was attractive, if a little tousled. When she caught sight of Clint and jumped back a little in surprise, the woman seemed even more attractive. Her wispy black hair was pinned back and was just mussed enough to look as though she'd recently rolled out of bed herself. Her dress was more of a nightgown. It didn't reveal much bare skin, but her breasts swung freely beneath the material.

"Oh, my," she yelped. "I didn't know anyone was standing there."

"Just an early riser," Clint said. "Didn't mean to sneak up on you."

"Well, breakfast won't be ready for a little while yet. If you'd like some coffee and fresh bread, I can fix you some of that."

"Actually, I'm getting pretty hungry. Anything I can do to help speed things along?"

She looked at him suspiciously at first, but then nodded. "You can start cracking eggs and then setting the table."

"I can do that." As he walked over to where a bowl of eggs was waiting, Clint introduced himself.

The woman's name was Sarah and she was married to the owner of the hotel. Before too long, they were talking back and forth and Sarah seemed to accept the fact that

Clint wasn't about to do much more than crack the eggs and set the table.

"So tell me," Clint said. "Have you heard anything about some miners who supposedly founded this town?"

"Are you joking?" When she saw Clint shake his head, she shrugged. "Then you really must be new to these parts. Everyone around here knows about them miners. Old bastards hated each other so much that they not only killed each other off, but insisted on being buried where they couldn't even see each other."

"That's what I heard in the saloon. I just didn't know if it was true."

"It's a tall tale, but true enough. I've seen the graves. If you were hearing stories in the saloon, you probably heard the one about the mine that's still supposed to be out there."

"Yeah," Clint said with a smirk. "I heard about that all right."

"That fella you were talking to last night knows all about that one." Sarah paused and glanced over her shoulder as if she thought Arthur might be standing behind her as well. When she saw nothing but the door behind her, she went on to say, "He's been after that mine for a while."

"How long?"

"Ever since he got to town about a year or so ago. He only started living here a few months back, but he pays his rent so that's where my concern ends. Is he a friend of yours?"

"Actually, he's my partner."

EIGHTEEN

Hearing one story didn't make it true.

Even getting a good gut feeling as well as some hard evidence didn't make that story true.

But hearing that same story verified by a whole tableful of folks over breakfast was enough to ease more than a few doubts in Clint's mind.

Over a hot plate of eggs, bread, and bacon, Clint heard half-a-dozen guests talk about the rumors going around about the lost mines. As they arrived to get their morning meal, they instantly joined in the conversation. Every last one of the people had at least a couple different things to add to the story. Surprisingly enough, Clint didn't hear too much that went against what Arthur had told him.

Some men would have written this off as coincidence. Others would have just credited it to a story that had been told enough times to be common knowledge. For Clint, it was one more thing to add to the feeling in his gut that he was doing the right thing.

One thing he learned for certain was that the story of the mines was powerful enough to keep men like Arthur interested in chasing them down. Clint knew for certain there were other interested parties who were more than willing to kill for a shot at those same mines. If nothing else, Arthur deserved to have someone watch his back while he took a stab of his own at the dream shared by an entire town.

Breakfast was still being served when Arthur made his appearance. He was scratching his head and yawning as he plopped into a chair and started in on his food. It didn't take long for him to get his wits about him and spot Clint sitting at another place at the table.

As soon as they saw him enter the room, the rest of the people having their breakfast stopped talking about the mines or anything that had to do with the founders of Scorpion's Tail. A few of them looked at Arthur warily, while some others plainly thought he was a few sandwiches short of a picnic.

"So what's the word?" Arthur asked.

Clint shrugged and replied, "The word is you're a late sleeper. I'll have to get going now. It was nice meeting all of you."

All of the guests said their good-byes and the middle-aged woman who'd cooked breakfast stood up to shake Clint's hand.

Arthur started shoveling the food into his mouth and guzzling his coffee so quickly that he was almost done with his meal by the time Clint had left the table.

Since he'd never really taken anything more than was necessary from his saddlebag, Clint was ready to go in a matter of minutes. When he walked out of his room, he almost ran straight into Arthur. The spindly man was carrying his own worn carpetbag by a pair of leather handles.

"So we're in business?" Arthur asked.

"Yeah, Arthur. We're in business. I figured since I couldn't let you just go out into the middle of nowhere to become a perfect target, watching out for you was the only way to keep my conscience clean."

"And the mines? You'll help look for the mines?"

"I'll help you while you're out there, but only on one condition."

"Sure, sure. What is it?"

"That I get the final say on when it's been too long and it's time to turn back."

His brow furrowed as Arthur asked, "What do you mean?"

"Men can waste the rest of their lives chasing after something that doesn't exist. Once you get out on your own, that becomes even easier to do. I admit there may be something to this whole legend, but you need to listen to me if I tell you that we're not doing anything out there besides chasing our own tails."

Arthur got a smirk on his face and gave Clint a nudge with his elbow. "You might get caught up in it too, you know."

"And if that happens, I'm sure you'll tell me it's time to let it be and head home. Is that a deal?"

"Watching out for each other is what partners do."

"And we'll listen if one decides the hunt is over," Clint said sternly. "That's the deal."

Nodding once and extending his hand sharply, Arthur said, "It's a deal."

"Fine then," Clint said as he grasped Arthur's hand and shook it with enough force to get the other man's undivided attention. "Let's go treasure hunting."

NINETEEN

As the sun rose and the day truly got its start, Clint's spirits couldn't help but take a turn for the better. Dawn had been cold and dim, making it seem closer to winter than it truly was. In the brightest hours of morning, however, Clint and Arthur had already collected their horses and were on their way to the starting point of their search.

The air had become crisp and clean, cooling them off instead of chilling them to the bone. Eclipse was always glad to be on the move rather than in a stable, no matter how good the accommodations were. Even Arthur's road-weary horse seemed to shed a few years as they put Scorpion's Tail behind them.

Considering the terrain, Clint was surprised that they could leave the town from more than two directions. The ledge that butted up against the town receded in spots that were hidden to the casual eye, making it only appear that the town had been built into a solid face of rock.

With Arthur anxiously leading the way, it didn't take long before they rounded a bend and spotted a small clearing just off the narrow trail. When he spotted it, Arthur stabbed his finger toward the clearing. "There it is, Clint. You see it?"

"I sure do."

"Not just the clearing. You see it?"

Clint squinted and leaned forward. After a moment or two, he was able to pick out something through the low-hanging branches and a thick carpet of dead leaves. It was a wooden cross sticking up out of the ground. "Yeah," he said again with more certainty. "I see it."

Before they even reached the clearing, Arthur had swung down from his saddle so he could jog up to the cross. His horse was either used to being left behind like that, or was out of steam anyway, because it took a few more steps before finding a patch of grass to occupy it.

Bringing Eclipse to a stop a little closer to where Arthur was now kneeling, Clint stayed in the saddle and took a look around. His eyes took careful inventory of the surrounding area before looking again at the cross. As far as he could tell, there wasn't anyone else approaching or waiting for them. Even so, he kept his guard up as he climbed down and walked over to Arthur's side.

"For being one of the founders of that town," Clint mused, "this grave sure isn't kept up too well."

"It used to be when the families came by to bury them. After that, folks let it slip."

Of course, there wasn't much to tend. All that could be seen to mark the last resting spot of this particular miner was two old boards lashed together. The only decoration was a name carved into one of those boards.

"Henry Obred Josefson," Clint read aloud. "That's our man."

Arthur brushed off the cross lovingly. "It sure is." After taking a silent moment for himself, Arthur dug into his pocket and removed his two valued clues. He looked down at them and when he looked up again, his face was bright enough to rival the sun shining through the ceiling of bare, crisscrossed branches.

"All right," Arthur said in a determined whisper. "All we

need to do now is figure out which of these clues marks the next step in the path."

Just then, Clint remembered what Arthur had said about there being other clues out there. Although there weren't many more to be found, there was the possibility that neither of the ones in Arthur's possession was the second one in the chain. Clint kept his reservations to himself, however, and put himself into more of a tracking frame of mind.

"All of these men were prospectors," he said. "They thought in terms of general direction and gut instinct."

Nodding while still studying the rock and arrowhead in his hand, Arthur said, "Yes, yes. Very true."

"All of this came together because of what you read in that town charter."

Clearly not paying attention, Arthur merely nodded and muttered, "Mmm-hmmm."

"Then maybe that was the first marker."

Arthur puttered around the cross and the ground surrounding it for another second or two before he straightened up and looked over at Clint. "I guess that would make sense."

"And if that's the first, then that would make this the second. Once you connect those two, that should at least point you in the right direction."

Looking back and forth between the cross and the town they'd left behind, Arthur finally smiled and nodded. "Exactly. That's exactly what I was about to tell you." As he walked past Clint to get back to his horse, Arthur patted him on the back. "I just might make a tracker out of you yet."

Clint lowered his head rather than say what was on his mind. When he did, he caught sight of something that he'd almost been flustered enough to miss.

Slowly, he crouched down and moved his hand just over the top of the leaves covering the ground. Clint retraced his as well as Arthur's steps through the clearing and around the grave. Luckily, neither of them had been there long enough to disturb everything. When he reached down to touch a partially clear spot amid the leaves, Clint pressed his fingertips down just hard enough to feel past the surface.

"Come on, Clint," Arthur yelled as he climbed into his saddle. "While we've still got the jump on the others who are looking for this trail."

A frown settled onto Clint's face as he got the shape of the spot he'd found and picked out several others that were roughly the same size. Although plenty of the spots had been wiped away when Arthur rushed over to get a look at the cross, there were still a few left that led in a direction that neither man had gone just yet.

Arthur still fretted like an overly anxious kid. "We're going to be the first ones to find those mines since the founders of Scorpion's Tail! I can feel it!"

But Clint knew it might already be too late for that. There was someone else already on that trail and they were ahead by at least a day.

TWENTY

One thing became obvious after less than an hour of riding with Arthur. No matter how well informed the spindly man might have been, or how much research he'd done, he would have gotten hopelessly lost in a matter of minutes if he hadn't had Clint to keep him on track.

They only had a general direction in which to go, but Arthur had trouble following even that simple guidance. More than once, Arthur almost steered his horse right back toward town, or even straight into a tangle of branches that might have caused his poor old horse to break its neck.

Clint saw all of this as a blessing of sorts. At least with Arthur's sense of direction, it was that much easier to lead him to where he needed to go rather than where he wanted to go.

Arthur wanted to go along the old miners' trail.

To stay alive, however, he needed to skirt around that trail and get a look at who was on it ahead of him. Clint kept this last part to himself as he calmly led Arthur toward that very purpose. All the while, Arthur kept right on talking as though he was on a holiday.

"So anyway," Arthur went on, "when Henry figured out

that the others weren't quite so loyal as when they'd left the hills, I say he should have known better than to—"

"Stop," Clint interrupted sharply.

Arthur looked confused for a moment before asking, "Stop riding or stop talking?"

"Both. Just stop. Now."

Pulling back on his reins, Arthur somehow managed to halt his story as well. Clint had no doubt that it would be picked up at the first opportunity at the exact spot where it had been halted.

But Clint wasn't worried about that just yet. While getting Arthur to stop talking so quickly was a sort of victory of its own, it wasn't the reason he'd brought them both to a standstill. Clint squinted as though he was staring at something, but wasn't exactly looking at one thing in particular. Instead, he was focusing more on what he could hear. The moment he heard Arthur start to ask a question, he stopped it with a quickly raised finger.

The wind was making its way through the trees, rattling all the dead leaves along the way. In the distance, running water could be heard. A few birds cried out, but they were a long way from Clint's spot.

Just when he was about to signal for Arthur to move on, he heard the sound that had made him call for a stop in the first place.

It was a subdued huffing sound that could very easily fall in with the rest of the noises. But there was also a deep rustling that went along with it. Now that he'd heard the sounds again, Clint had a good idea of which direction they were coming from.

Dropping his voice to a low whisper, Clint looked over to Arthur and said, "Stay here. I'll be right back."

"Where are you—" Arthur stopped short when he got an angry glare from Clint. He then dropped his own voice to the same whisper and asked, "Where are you going?"

Rather than say anything Clint pointed to the path ahead

of them and then made a half-circle motion. He dropped silently from the saddle, pressing his feet down firmly when he hit the ground to keep the crunch of dead leaves as quiet as possible. When he saw that Arthur was about to say something else, Clint headed him off by explaining, "There's someone out there."

That got Arthur to clamp his mouth shut and shrink down into his saddle. The color drained from his face as his eyes started darting nervously back and forth.

Clint reached for the rifle slung on the side of his saddle and handed it over to Arthur. "Can you use this?"

"Y-yes. I should be able to manage."

The answer wasn't too convincing, but it would have to do. After handing off the rifle, Clint crouched down and started moving away from the trail.

Eclipse needed less instruction than Arthur in how to behave. The Darley Arabian remained where he was, keeping his feet planted and his eyes on Clint. Even when Clint disappeared into some of the surrounding trees, the stallion lowered his head and waited patiently.

Arthur, on the other hand, got nervous the moment Clint was out of his sight. He strained his ears to hear Clint's steps, but soon lost the sound of them. His hands started to sweat around the rifle, sending the chill up through his arms and into his entire body.

Before he could get too jittery, he heard the footsteps returning. Arthur let out his breath and watched for Clint to reappear. That was when he realized the steps weren't Clint's.

That is, they weren't unless Clint had figured out a way to approach from three directions at once.

TWENTY-ONE

"Out for a ride?" came a voice from the trees.

As Arthur looked around nervously, his hands tensed around the rifle and started to shake. For a moment, it seemed it was only a matter of time before he dropped the weapon. Somehow he not only managed to keep hold of it, but he even levered in a fresh round.

"Why don't you show yourselves?" Arthur half-asked and half-demanded.

"Certainly," said a different voice to his left.

The first one who'd spoken came out of the trees almost directly in front of Arthur. Now that he could put a face to the voice, Arthur was shown that his first guess concerning the speaker had been correct.

"You're a lady," he said in relief. And just as quickly as he'd lowered the gun, he brought it back up again. "Why are you surrounding me? Who's with you?"

Arthur was correct about one thing. The rider ahead of him was most definitely a lady. She sat in the saddle like she was born there, shifting her hips with every motion of the animal beneath her. She wore the rugged clothes of a cowboy, but with a jacket that had just a hint of femininity.

Short fringes shook back and forth as she moved, reminding Arthur of the hem of a dancing girl's dress.

Long, wavy, chestnut-brown hair flowed over her shoulders. Although it was tied off into two separate tails, her hair was thick enough to almost come together at her back. Her hat was made from battered leather, complete with a silver band.

Once Arthur was done taking the sight of her in, his eyes finally took notice of the guns strapped around her waist.

As if sensing his skittishness, the lady raised her gloved hands and gave him a friendly smile. "No need to point any guns. We've just met."

Arthur glanced to his left at the other rider who'd come forward. This one was almost as skinny as Arthur was, but seemed more wiry. He gripped his reins in one hand while holding a pistol across his lap with the other.

Just as the man was going to say something, a hand darted out from the trees so quickly that it closed around his leg before the wiry fellow even knew it was there. He tried to bring the gun around, but was already on his way out of the saddle before he could do anything about it. He landed flat on his back, forcing all the air from his lungs in a solid, wheezing huff.

By the time the man blinked away the fog from his eyes and sucked in half a breath, he was staring up at the wrong end of a modified Colt. Behind it, Clint looked down at him and winked.

"Howdy," Clint said. Looking up at another section of trees, he added, "You heard the lady. No need for guns. Might as well toss yours down so we can introduce ourselves properly."

Although she looked surprised by Clint's appearance, the lady didn't look too rattled. Rather than toss her gun down, she made sure to keep her hands well away from it as she set them flat upon her knees.

Arthur was still staring down the rifle. He nearly jumped back out of his saddle when he heard the rustle of branches to his right. There came the sound of heavy footsteps, followed by a lighter rustle and then the solid thump as a pistol came through the air to land on the ground.

Clint eased up on the man he'd taken down.

"Are there more of them?" Arthur asked.

"Nope," Clint said while offering a hand to the man on the ground. "Just the three."

The wiry man on the ground started to get up and winced at the effort of pulling in a breath. His next breath came more easily. As he got to his feet, he slapped away Clint's hand and struggled up on his own.

"What brings you out this morning?" the lady asked.

Clint looked over at her and made sure it was a good look. She had a fire to her that made it seem as though she was in charge no matter what was going on. At the very least, she looked like she could handle whatever came her way. Before too long, Clint realized that he might have a hard time looking away if he didn't do so quickly.

"We're just headed into the mountains," Clint said. "There have been some robbers around here, so we're a bit jumpy."

The subtle shift in her smile made it clear that the lady wasn't buying that for a moment. Even so, she nodded and said, "We've run into some trouble on that front as well. Maybe we should ride together."

Hearing that, Arthur snapped his eyes toward Clint as he started spewing out a series of panicked syllables. "I don't . . . that is . . . we shouldn't . . . I mean it wouldn't be . . ."

"What my friend's trying to say is that we wouldn't want to impose."

The lady nodded to each of her companions in turn. "Seems like we already got the worst of it out of our systems. Might as well share some company on such a beauti-

ful day. Besides, folks need all the help they can get in
these mountains."

Going by the look on Clint's face, one might have
thought that he wasn't thinking about anything more important than the weather. There was plenty more going on
inside his thoughts, however, but that didn't mean he had to
show them on his sleeve.

"I don't ride with anyone I don't know," Clint said
sternly. After a tense second or two, he let a smile onto his
face as he added, "So we should get to know each other.
My name's Clint."

When he saw the expectant look he was getting from
Clint, Arthur gave up on what he'd been trying to say.
"Arthur," he sighed. "Pleased to meet you."

Bringing her horse a bit closer to where Clint was
standing, the lady reached down with one hand and said,
"I'm Eve. The fellow you pulled out of the saddle is Emmett and that sour-looking fellow behind me is Vernon."

"No hard feelings, I hope," Clint said to Emmett.

Emmett put on a surprisingly friendly smile and replied,
"Could've been a lot worse. Just make sure it don't happen
again."

"It's a deal." Now Clint turned and accepted Eve's hand.
Her grip was firm, but not overpowering. Now that she was
closer, he got a better look into her brilliant, green eyes.
"This should be interesting."

Eve nodded and leaned back into her saddle after shaking Clint's hand. "I certainly hope so."

TWENTY-TWO

The newly formed group of five riders worked their way into an increasingly tangled batch of trees. Their first impulse was to remain close to the ones they knew, which meant Eve, Vernon, and Emmett stuck close to each other while Clint and Arthur stuck together as well. Both groups talked among themselves now and then, but the trail they were on wasn't exactly easy going.

A narrow path could barely be seen through the fallen branches and dead leaves. Even when that path was perfectly visible, it wound through large trees and skirted close to rocky ledges that had drop-offs ranging from shallow ditches to steep slides up to a hundred yards deep.

At times, the riders had to go single-file so they could keep an eye on each other while also keeping an eye on the trail ahead of them. It was at a time like that when Arthur brought his horse up close to Eclipse so he could whisper without being heard by the others.

Making sure to keep the other three in his sight, Arthur leaned over a bit and hissed, "I don't like this, Clint. Not one bit."

"Yeah," Clint said in a voice that wasn't a whisper, but

was still low enough to travel no farther than where he wanted it to go. "I kind of figured that out already."

"Why would you do this? You know we're supposed to be looking for . . . well, you know what we're looking for. Kane's out there and Lord only knows who else knows about it from him. We need to find this on our own and the fewer people who know about it the better."

Clint had to smile and shake his head as he listened to Arthur's tirade. Even though the man kept his voice down, he was still managing to build himself up into a frenzy. His words might not have carried too far, but his voice was like the hiss of steam being pushed through a piston. The sound of that was drawing a few backward glances, but not much else. At least, not yet.

"What are we supposed to do when we have to turn a different way?" Arthur asked. "What do we say? How do we explain what we're doing?"

"Hey!" Clint shouted.

The sound of his voice was loud enough to catch the attention of the other three and almost enough to knock Arthur from his saddle. After whispering so intently, the shock of hearing Clint wedged the rest of what Arthur meant to say squarely in the middle of his throat.

Although Clint was watching Arthur from the corner of his eye, he was staring ahead at Eve. The lady turned in her saddle in response to the shout and brought her horse to a stop.

"We'll be circling around off this trail for a bit," Clint said to her. "We'll catch up with you later."

She nodded, gave him a wave, and flicked her reins again. Emmett and Vernon did the same.

After leading Arthur off the trail just far enough to be out of the others' sight, Clint brought Eclipse to a stop and said, "There. Does that set that concern to rest?"

Arthur glanced nervously back and forth between Clint

and the trail where they'd left the other three. Reluctantly, he grumbled, "I guess so. But that still doesn't answer my question. Why agree to ride with anyone else when we need to keep our business quiet?"

"Because," Clint replied in a steady, even tone, "there were others at that gravestone not too long before we were. Three others to be exact. Since I don't have a love for coincidences, I'm pretty sure those three were the ones. I also think that if they were there, heading in the same direction we were and looking over their shoulders like us, then they're probably on the same trail as us."

"Good Lord," Arthur said. He blinked quickly and looked back and forth as though he was expecting to be ambushed at any second. "Good Lord, I think you're right."

Keeping his voice low, but shifting it to a tone meant to calm Arthur down a bit, Clint said, "I figure they were at that grave less than a day before we got there. Could be less depending on the weather, the wind, or any number of things. Since they were close enough to hear us, they ether hadn't moved on too far just yet or they were keeping an eye out for anyone else visiting that grave who seemed to want more than just a look at some of Scorpion Tail's history."

"You think they work for Kane?"

Clint squinted and mulled that over. "Hard to say. So far, this Kane fellow seems to be more the type to try and kill us first and then move on. Actually, that's what I was expecting when I took their offer."

"You mean you thought they might try to kill us?" Arthur blinked in disbelief. At the moment, that was about all he could do. "What if there were more of them?"

"I looked and didn't find any more. The point is, if they meant to try something, it's best to be able to see them when it happens. That's also why I agreed to ride with them for a while. Better to keep them in our sights and split off when we need to."

"But if we see something important, that'll tip them off too."

"Not if we let it pass, split off later, and then double back."

It took a few moments for Arthur to see the sense behind Clint's thinking, but when he found it he put on a beaming smile. "That's pretty smart."

"I have my moments. Isn't this why you wanted me along?"

"I guess so. Still, I don't want them to know what we're after."

"That's what I've been trying to tell you. It's too late for that. They're after it too. All we can do now is make sure that if there is something out there to find, we're the first ones to find it."

Clint saw the conflict in Arthur's eyes. He could almost hear the battle between greed and common sense in the spindly man's brain. To help tip the balance, Clint added, "You know there's other clues out there, right?"

"Certainly."

"And if these three are after those mines, then they probably have one of those clues for themselves. Following them might just help us."

This time, Arthur didn't need to think about what he'd heard. Those words seemed to hit the nail right on the head. "Now that's what I call thinking."

Clint tapped his temple and snapped his reins. As he'd figured, the other three hadn't gotten too far ahead of them.

TWENTY-THREE

Clint didn't hurry to catch up with Eve, Vernon, and Emmett. He didn't need to. All it took was some steady riding at a constant pace and soon the other three horses came into view. By that time, Arthur had calmed down a bit. He was still jittery enough to hold his tongue once he caught sight of the three riders on the trail ahead.

All in all, Clint figured things were going better than they had in a while.

Whether he could trust those other three or not, Clint was playing in a game where most of the cards were on the table. There would always be some surprises lurking in the shadows, but every high-stakes game had some of those.

Not too long after they'd met up again, the riders started mingling together. The trail had widened up a bit and even flattened somewhat. There were still high rock walls on one side and thick trees on the other, but at least they didn't have to watch every step their horses took.

Vernon took the position up front, while Arthur and Emmett took to riding side by side. Once they found a mutual interest, they both started swapping stories and chattering back and forth. Meanwhile, Eve's horse had drifted closer to Clint. Although he wasn't sure just how intentional that was, he did know that it saved him the trouble of steering Eclipse toward her.

"So," Clint said as he looked over to Eve. "What sort of business brings you out in this country?"

"We took a job from a prospecting company," she told him. "Following up on some old claims, updating records, that sort of thing."

"Trying to make a lucky strike?"

"Nothing quite like that. Some of these old miners file a claim and expect it to hold up even though nobody hears from them for years. Plenty of others want to contest the claim, so people like us need to go out and see if anyone's still working it or if it's been abandoned without anyone hearing about it."

"Sounds fascinating."

Eve let out a short laugh and replied, "Then you must not have been listening to me. It's boring as hell. Just a lot of riding around, trying to follow directions that use oddly shaped stumps or some kind of rock formation as the only landmarks. I swear, if any of these old-timers actually used a real map, my job would be so much easier."

"Seems like it would take a lot more than that to make your job easier."

"What makes you say that?" Eve asked.

"This part of the country must be cut up into more claims than I could imagine. Checking them out one by one sounds like a tough job."

"It is. Of course, there are some parts of Arizona and California that are a whole lot worse. Also, I don't need to check on all of them. Just the claims that are being contested. There's no reason to check on the rest. What about you, Clint?"

"I'm out here on a job as well."

"Both of you?"

"Not quite. He's the one with the business," Clint said, hooking a thumb back toward Arthur. "I'm just here to make sure he doesn't get himself into too much trouble."

"Sounds like a tougher job than mine."

"Really? Than you must know Arthur pretty well."

"I've heard of him," she said with an easy laugh.

"Seeing as how much he likes to talk, you've probably heard him a few miles outside of Scorpion's Tail."

"Just about. At least that's something he and Emmett have in common."

Sure enough, those two were still in the middle of a heated discussion that neither man seemed willing to budge on. Still, despite all the animation in their gestures while they ranted to one another, both men seemed to be having the time of their lives.

"Let them talk," Clint said, turning back around in his saddle. "Maybe they'll run out of steam so we won't have to listen to them for a while."

Eve laughed at that and turned her attention to the road ahead. So far, there wasn't much to see. Clint knew that for certain because he'd been keeping his eyes open for anything that might catch his attention while also having something to do with one of the clues Arthur had mentioned.

It only made sense to him that the clues would have to work that way. Not only did prospectors and mountain men think in terms of landmarks, but they were supposedly marking the path for their families to follow on their own. Therefore, it stood to reason that with the clues in mind, the landmarks wouldn't be too hard to miss.

Eve's voice was like a rush of warm water over his skin. It flowed by, soothing him as it went. While he enjoyed talking to her and seeing her smile, he wasn't about to let himself be pulled too far from his own course. He could tell that she was doing the same thing that he was.

As she conversed with him about any number of topics, her eyes would occasionally shift over from one place to another. She kept a close watch over the land around her as well as her two companions. Although Emmett seemed to be engrossed in his own conversation with Arthur, Vernon shifted around in his saddle every now and then to send Eve a meaningful glance.

One such glance caught Clint's attention. Not that it was so much different than the others, but more from the effect it had upon Eve when she caught it. Something shifted subtly in her bearing. There was a new urgency in her eyes that hadn't been there before.

She glanced to the right and then put on another little smile. "One of those claims I needed to check should be coming up here before long. Maybe tonight we could meet up again? Emmett brought along some nice strips of beef."

"And Arthur brews a hell of a cup of coffee."

"It's settled then. Just tell me where you two will—"

A gunshot cracked through the air.

Clint's hand dropped reflexively to his Colt as he twisted in his saddle to see where the shot had come from. He was just in time to see Emmett fall from his horse.

TWENTY-FOUR

Emmett hit the ground on his side. He gritted his teeth and let out a pained grunt as his ribs pounded against the rocky soil. His horse reared a bit and backed off, more spooked by the fact that his rider had dropped than by what had dropped him.

Arthur's mouth was open in shock, but soon he was grasping for the pistol stuck under his belt.

"Son of a bitch," Vernon grunted as he brought his own horse around so he was facing the rest of the party. With one motion, he pulled the rifle from its holster on his saddle and was preparing it to fire.

Clint and Eve both had the same idea in drawing their weapons and turning so they could get a better look at the trees surrounding them on one side. Although someone could very likely have taken up a position in the rocks on the other side, they'd both heard enough to know that the shot had come from the trees.

Although both he and Eve had gotten their guns out and ready fairly quickly, there was still one major problem. Neither of them had a target.

"Arthur!" Clint shouted. "Get off that horse and get on the ground."

Arthur seemed stunned, but did as he was told. It was unclear as to whether his dismount had been purposeful or just some act of divine clumsiness. Either way, he was out of the line of fire for the moment.

"You all right, Emmett?" Clint asked.

Eve was backing her horse toward Vernon. As her eyes scanned the area around them, she asked, "Did you see who fired that shot?"

Vernon shook his head. "I heard some movement in the trees, but didn't get a chance to say anything about it before that shot came."

"There's bound to be more of them. Clint, what are you doing?"

Hunkering down low over Eclipse's neck, Clint draped his gun arm over the stallion's neck and started giving orders in a calm whisper. The Darley Arabian responded perfectly, lowering his head and allowing Clint to slide down to the ground.

"Emmett," Clint said as he got closer to the fallen man. "Are you hurt?"

Emmett was wrapped in several layers of thick, dark cotton ranging from a dirty pair of brown pants to his old shirt and the brown coat that went over all of it. With all of that bunched around him, it was difficult to tell if he was laying properly or if he'd busted a leg on impact.

When he flopped onto his back, his face was twisted in a pained mask. He looked a lot older up close than when Clint had seen him the first time. Of course, falling out of the saddle twice in one day had a tendency to age a man beyond his years.

"Nothing's broken," Emmett said in a strained voice. "Maybe I'm just getting used to this."

"Here," Clint said, offering his hand. When Emmett took it, Clint hoisted the man onto his feet. He held on after that to make sure Emmett had his footing. Letting go bit by bit, he saw that the man was a bit wobbly but managing to stay up on his own.

"Take your horse and follow Arthur onto the trail," Clint ordered.

When the other two men moved past him, Clint brought Eclipse into a position at the back of the group. He looked back to see that Vernon was still at the front and Eve was already moving toward the middle.

Before they could complete their formation, another shot came at them. This one hissed through the air past Clint's head. It wasn't close enough to do any damage, but it was still way too close for his liking.

"That's another shooter," Eve said.

Vernon nodded once and brought the rifle up to his shoulder. Pivoting in his saddle, he drew a bead and squeezed his trigger. Not only did the bullet rattle some branches as it flew through the air, but it caused something else to rattle even more bushes as it dived for cover.

Still sighting down his rifle, Vernon said, "Make that three."

Clint caught sight of something moving to his right. The instant he saw the flicker of sunlight off of bared iron, he aimed and took a shot. Even though he couldn't get a good look at who was doing the shooting, Clint was able to make a good enough guess as to where he could fire without hitting much.

The Colt spit its round through the air, carving a tunnel through the tree branches and sending a shower of leaves to the ground in its wake. Judging by the burst of motion that came after the shot, Clint had done just what he'd set out to do. No man could run that fast if he was hurt.

Eve and Vernon were keeping busy as well. They fired off their shots as a few more came in from the trees. While they were sending more rounds into the bushes compared to the few that came their way, Eve and Vernon were the ones who were being forced off their horses. It wasn't long after that before they were forced even closer to the ground.

"They're closing in on us," Eve said.

Vernon was down on one knee and sighting down his rifle in a classic shooter's stance. Another shot exploded from the trees, clipping him in the shoulder. A chunk of his jacket flew away, accompanied by a thin spray of blood. The man didn't do more than twitch in response to it, however. Instead, he readjusted his aim and took another shot.

"Close ranks," Clint said. "Put your backs to the rocks."

Waiting until the others started following his orders, Clint forced himself to keep his eyes on the trees. When he couldn't hold back another instant, he turned his entire upper body around until he was forced to drop onto his back.

Sure enough, when he took that sudden look behind and up, he saw a rifleman nestled up in those rocks. The man leaned out to get a better aim, taking his time to decide which back he wanted to put a bullet through first.

Clint's shoulders hadn't even hit the dirt before he brought his Colt around and aimed at the rifleman as though he was just pointing him out with one finger. He pulled the trigger, causing the Colt to buck against his palm and slam his shoulders down against the ground.

For a moment, Clint wasn't sure if he'd hit him or not. Digging out a rifleman in a position like that was tricky business. There were precious few opportunities to take a shot and one miss would whittle those chances down to almost nothing.

The rifleman's head poked out from where he'd been hiding, soon to be followed by the rest of his body as he fell forward and toppled to the ground. His gun fell with him, both twisting through the air like baggage clumsily dropped from a stage's roof until they hit the ground just behind Emmett and Arthur.

Reflexively, Arthur turned around and shot at the noise from behind him. Apparently, he'd been looking the wrong way or covering his eyes completely when Clint had fired his gun. The shot sparked against the rocks, causing him to jump again.

More and more rounds were sparking against the rocks, but these were coming from the gunmen in the trees. Clint saw that Eve and Vernon were doing their best to make themselves as small a target as possible, but even those options were dwindling by the second. Both of them were laying on their bellies and sending their shots into the trees whenever they could.

Arthur snapped himself around, holding his pistol in trembling hands. The pistol slapped against something solid and didn't budge another inch. When Arthur opened his eyes, he saw a hand wrapped around his gun and Clint crouching beside him.

"Give me this," Clint said while plucking the gun from Arthur's shaky grasp and reloading that as well as his own Colt.

"What are you doing?" Arthur whined. "They'll be on us any second!"

With a gun in each hand, Clint faced the trees and said, "I know. They seemed to have planned this pretty well. Let's see if they expect this."

Pulling in a deep breath, Clint launched himself toward the trees.

TWENTY-FIVE

Clint's boots pounded against the dirt like a one-man stampede. He fired a shot or two in front of him until he steered himself in the direction he wanted to go. Once there, Clint lowered his head and rushed into the inferno with both guns blazing.

Every step thundered in his ears almost as loudly as the fire erupting from his fists. He made it to the tree line in no time at all, and was soon twisting his body to avoid the branches. Lead hissed past him like angry hornets, but Clint merely shrugged it off and moved on.

It was too late to worry about getting hit now. He knew a move like this was similar to pushing everything you had into the middle of a poker table. Once you took that step, all that remained was to follow it through to the end.

Clint caught sight of his first real target the moment he stepped off the trail and into the trees. It was a single figure standing with his back pressed against a solid trunk. Although the gunman took a shot at Clint out of reflex, the shock he felt was clearly written all over his face. After that shot, he turned tail and ran for better cover, firing wildly over his shoulder.

Clint still ran forward, holding both guns at waist level

and sending out a wave of lead that ripped bark off of trees and drew more than its share of blood.

Men leapt from cover as they would in front of a charging bull. Although some of them began to make a stand, the fire in Clint's eyes shone through and they were all soon backing off.

All this time, Clint was only thinking about two things: how deep into the trees he was running and how many bullets he had left. It wouldn't be long before he reached his limits on both counts, but it seemed that he would make it there alive and well.

Slowing himself down to a jog, Clint dropped Arthur's gun into his holster and then snapped open the cylinder of his Colt. He didn't even have to look at what he was doing as he dropped out the empty shells and replaced them with fresh rounds from his gun belt. Clint's eyes were searching the trees for any sign of a straggler.

As far as he could tell, the only thing that hadn't run away was a deer that had been petrified and rooted to its spot. Given this lull in gunfire, even that animal took the opportunity to turn tail and get the hell out of there.

Rather than count his blessings just yet, Clint lowered himself as close to the ground as he could go without actually dropping to his knees. His senses stretched out to take in everything he could, but even that wasn't very much.

After all the shooting, the air among the trees was filled with a veil of dark smoke that formed a layer of grit in Clint's mouth. His ears were still ringing from the shots, but he was accustomed to that enough to be able to push through it and search for another kind of sound.

As much as he searched, however, Clint didn't find what he was after. The only thing he could hear was the occasional footstep as it crunched on some leaves while getting away from him.

Just to be sure, Clint sent another three shots into the biggest trees he could see. Since nothing stirred around or behind any of them, he figured his job was done. Heading back to where he'd left the others, Clint reloaded the Colt once again and snapped the cylinder shut as he stepped onto the trail.

He wasn't startled by the gun barrels pointed at him. In fact, those were the reason why he'd been certain to lower his gun before stepping into the open. "It's all right," Clint said. "It's just me."

Eve and Vernon let out their breaths and lowered their weapons.

"How many are out there?" Eve asked.

"I figure it couldn't have been more than half a dozen or so. Maybe less. Either way, they're gone now."

Vernon looked toward the trees and then back to Clint. "You sure about that?"

Clint nodded. "Whoever didn't run would have had enough sand to charge us earlier or take me out as soon as I came at them. They're gone, but I'm sure they'll be back."

It was only now that Eve seemed to truly let her guard down a bit. Her shoulders lowered a little and she got back onto both feet. "Who the hell was that?"

"What do you think?" Clint asked while looking back at Arthur. "Does this seem like Kane's style?"

Clint didn't get an answer from Arthur, but he was no longer looking at him to see what was keeping him quiet. Instead, Clint was getting a look at Eve and Vernon to see how they reacted to his question.

Vernon didn't say anything, although the name Clint had mentioned didn't seem to take him by surprise.

Something flashed across Eve's face that made her look back toward the trees. She didn't give an answer either, but between her and Vernon's reactions, Clint got more than enough of an answer from them both.

Eve holstered her pistol and walked toward the crumpled body of the fallen rifleman. Without much of a reaction to the bloodied, broken corpse, she pushed it onto its back with her toe and took a long look at his face. After a moment of studying the face, which was covered with dirt and blood, she shook her head.

"I don't recognize him," she said. "What about any of you?"

Vernon walked over and looked down at the body. Compared to his reaction, Eve's was downright emotional. His eyes shifted down to the corpse as though he was looking at something that had dropped out of his pocket.

After staring into the rifleman's gaping eyes, Vernon shook his head. "Never seen him."

"Come over here, Arthur," Clint said.

Arthur didn't move. His voice drifted toward the others like a stray bit of wind. "He's dead."

"I know he's dead, Arthur, but I need you to come and see if you recognize him."

"No, not him," Arthur replied. "It's Emmett. He's dead."

TWENTY-SIX

Clint, Eve, and Vernon all rushed over to where Arthur was huddled on the ground. But Arthur wasn't just huddled to cover his head or keep himself down. He was hunching down protectively over Emmett's unmoving body.

"Oh, no," Eve said softly. Reaching down, Eve's hand was steady at first, but began to tremble slightly just before she touched Emmett's shoulder. She took hold of him and gently eased him onto his back.

Emmett had been laying mostly on one side as if he was just about to flop onto his belly. When he was rolled onto his back, he let out a subtle wheeze as the last bit of breath from his lungs escaped into the air. His eyes were open wide. A surprised look was etched onto his face.

"I think I heard something," Arthur said hopefully. "Maybe he's—"

Clint stopped him with a hand on his shoulder. Partly to keep him back while he and Eve got a closer look, and partly because he already knew what they were going to find.

Eve leaned down as though she was listening to whispered words coming from Emmett's mouth. When she moved her head away from him, she reached down and eased Emmett's eyes closed. She then looked to the others gathered around and shook her head.

"He's gone," she said.

But Clint didn't need to be told that much. While everyone else was looking at Emmett's face, he'd been looking at the bloody wounds that had brought him down. Emmett's forearm had been torn open and was twisted around his body at an odd angle. A dark stain had spread over the front of his chest, with a wet hole in the middle of it.

Clint backed up a step and found Vernon right there. Although he still had next-to-no expression on his face, Vernon was expending a lot of effort to keep it that way.

"We need to get moving," Vernon said. "Clint might have scared them off a bit, but they'll circle back around soon enough."

Eve nodded as she stood up. "I agree. This was a perfect spot for an ambush and we were lucky to make it out at all. We'd be stupid to wait around and give them another chance."

As much as Clint agreed with them, he didn't say so right away. Instead, he walked over to Arthur and offered a hand to help the man back onto his feet. "Come on, Arthur. We need to go."

Arthur's eyes remained fixed upon Emmett. While there was some sadness in his expression, that seemed to be overshadowed by the pure shock that was flooding through his entire system. When he finally looked up at Clint, Arthur seemed like he'd just been shaken out of a deep sleep.

"We were just talking," Arthur said. "I can still hear his voice."

Clint nodded and led Arthur away from one body and toward the other. "I know. But he's gone now and we've got to get moving too. First, take a look at this man."

Since he was already pretty far gone, Arthur didn't seem overly shocked to look down at the dead rifleman. He gazed down at the corpse without seeing it for a few moments until he finally felt Clint give him a little bit of a shake.

"Come on now," Clint prodded. "Take a look and tell me what you see. There'll be time for the rest later."

Arthur blinked and rubbed the heel of his hand against his eyes. Letting out a breath, he took another look. After a second or two, he leaned down a bit so he could study the face even harder. When he pulled himself back, he nodded and said, "I've seen him. I don't know his name, but I've seen him."

"Is he one of Kane's men?" Clint asked.

Once again, Arthur nodded. He didn't have enough left in him to say or do much else.

Clint pulled Arthur to his horse and stayed put until the man had climbed into the saddle. From there, Clint drew the pistol from his holster and stuck it under Arthur's belt. He then dropped his Colt back into his own holster where it belonged.

Vernon was already on his horse. "Everyone ready to go?"

Arthur was dazed, but had his reins in hand. "What about Emmett? We can't just leave him there."

Eve had taken the reins to Emmett's horse and was leading it off the road. "I'll see to him," she said. "The rest of you go on ahead and I'll catch up."

Before anyone else could say anything more, Clint went over to Emmett's body and hefted it over one shoulder. "Go on," he said to Vernon. "We won't be long."

TWENTY-SEVEN

Vernon and Arthur rode at a slow pace for less than half an hour before they heard the rumble of hooves coming up from behind them. Vernon twisted in his saddle with one hand resting on the rifle across his lap. He didn't relax that gun arm until he spotted both Eve and Clint as the approaching riders.

Although they eased up a bit, neither Clint nor Eve slowed to anywhere close to the speed that the other two were going. Instead, they waved their hands in a motion to follow. Vernon responded instantly, slapping the flank of Arthur's horse before giving his own reins a snap.

All four riders headed down the trail before branching off once the terrain opened up a bit. Once the spot of the ambush was a mile and a half behind them, Clint signaled for the group to slow down.

As they slowed to a trot, they searched the area around them and found no cause for concern. Rather than allow himself to relax, Clint reached into his saddlebag and pulled out the dented spyglass that was one of his constant companions.

He lifted the lens to his eye and rechecked the terrain. Focusing in on something to the northeast, Clint nodded and said, "They're still moving."

"You sure that's them?" Vernon asked.

"Pretty sure. Looks to be about half a dozen of them and most are carrying rifles. Other than that, I can't see too much more."

"That's good enough for me," Eve said as she let out a relieved breath. "It should be good enough to get us a few hours of peace anyway. What do you think, Vernon?"

The other man scowled in the direction that Clint was looking. He'd since gotten out his own spyglass and was studying the riders Clint had pointed out. Finally, he lowered the spyglass and dropped it into his bag. "It'll have to do for now. That is," he added hopefully, "unless you want to take off after them."

"Maybe later," Eve said. "Let's not forget why we're here."

"And why's that?" Arthur asked.

Eve shifted around to look at him as if she'd forgotten Arthur was even there. "Excuse me?"

"You don't seem too surprised to be attacked like that," Arthur said. "What kind of claims are you checking on anyway?"

When she looked over to Clint, all Eve got from him was a nod.

"Sounds like a good question to me," Clint told her.

"Things can get rough, Clint. You know that." Eve shook her head and flicked her reins so she didn't have to sit still under the scrutiny of the other two. "I'm not the one who those gunmen were after anyway. You've got your friend to blame for that one. Besides, who's this Jervis Kane you were talking about? That's something else I'd like to discuss once we find a safe place to make camp."

Even though he'd been anxious for a fight before, Vernon didn't much appreciate having that fight spread among his own people. Clearly aggravated, he said, "If we're looking to find a campsite, then let's get to it. There'll be plenty of time to scrap then, because right now we're just giving those assholes a good look at us as well as plenty of time to circle around."

"He's right," Clint said. "We need to get moving and get out of the open."

But Arthur was still glaring at Eve. His gaze was so intense that it brought her around to glare right back at him.

For a moment, it seemed that the war of words would start anew between them. Instead, they both turned away and let their emotions bleed into the cold wind that had started whipping around their heads. Eve snapped her reins hard and took off, soon to be followed by Vernon.

Clint rode Eclipse back to circle around next to Arthur. Reaching out, he set a calming hand on Arthur's arm. "You'll feel better once we get moving. Just try to think about that for now."

"I'll try, Clint," Arthur said weakly. "It's just that, I've never been around so much killing."

"You could always forget about this business and head back. Nobody would blame you if—"

"No, Clint. I'm not turning back. I've come too far for that."

No matter how rattled Arthur was, it was plain to see that he meant those words with every fiber of his being. Come to think of it, Clint had yet to see Arthur actually run away from anything so far. He might have ducked, whined, fretted, or hid, but he hadn't run away.

"Reload that pistol," Clint said. "And start keeping it somewhere you can get to it when you need it. You don't even want to think about what you might lose if that thing goes off when it's stuck under your belt."

Arthur looked down and winced. Following through on Clint's orders kept him busy for a while after that.

TWENTY-EIGHT

Although they did a good stretch of riding, they didn't stray too far from the spot of the ambush. After circling around and backtracking for a while, Eve pointed toward a cluster of large boulders. There were some trees and plenty of shrubs scattered around the boulders, which suited everyone just fine.

"This'll do," Vernon said. "With these rocks at our backs, anyone who wants to try and jump us will either have to climb over them or walk through these leaves and dry branches."

Nodding, Clint said, "Either way, we'll hear them coming."

"Exactly."

"We'll have to keep our fire small, though, or we might wind up cooking ourselves instead of dinner."

"Fire?" Vernon asked. "You want to advertise we're here?"

"Either that or freeze. It's going to get cold overnight."

"Better cold than dead."

Coming up on the other side of Vernon, Eve slapped his shoulder and said, "We'll keep a small fire. Anyone who's been watching us knows we're camped here. That's why I looked so hard to find a spot that's hard to sneak into."

"There's always more riflemen," Vernon said.

"And they'll be able to pick us off whether there's a fire or not," Eve replied. "We knew this wasn't going to be a picnic. Of course," she added while glancing over to Arthur, "we didn't know someone would be attracting the kind of firepower that we've been getting, but we'll just work with what we've got."

Arthur glanced back and forth, becoming less and less comfortable with every shift of his eyes. "I didn't mean to cause any trouble."

"Well, you might not have caused it, but you attract it all the same." Eve leaned forward, propping herself with one elbow upon the saddle. "You want to tell us any more about Jervis Kane?"

Clint had been bothered by something the last time this subject was brought up, and had been keeping it in the back of his head for another time. But he didn't like the way both Eve and Vernon were turning against the spindly man, so he figured now was as good a time as any.

Surprisingly enough, Arthur beat him to the punch when he said, "I think you know plenty about Kane."

"Is that so?"

"Yes, it is."

"And what makes you think that?"

"Because I've only mentioned his last name when I was talking to Clint."

Eve thought about that for a second and shrugged. "So, I've probably heard of him. In my line of work, I hear about plenty of bad men and this one is the worst one I've come across in a while. Now do we want to camp here or not?"

Clint swung down from his saddle and started taking his bedroll and supplies out. "This is perfect for me. With the way you two tend to bite at each other, I doubt there's many places we can go without attracting attention."

It was getting into the evening hours by the time they had camp set up and a place cleared away for a fire. Collecting wood was no problem, since avoiding burning all the fallen branches and leaves was their bigger concern. After getting an early start, they wound up with a comfortable little camp.

Vernon wasn't the type to sit still for long, so he set out to scout the area. Arthur busied himself with preparing supper, leaving Eve and Clint to walk the immediate area to make sure nobody was closing in on them.

"Beautiful country," Eve said after a long period of silence.

Clint looked around and saw the rugged terrain outlined in the dark reddish and purple hues of the sky at dusk. A chill was setting in, but by this time it had been a constant companion and Clint barely even felt it much anymore.

The Rockies were in the distance as always. Depending on the angle and time of day, they either seemed a week's ride away or close enough to touch.

"You're right about that," Clint said. His eyes had fallen more onto Eve when he said that, however. "Just beautiful."

The setting sun was creating streaks of lighter brown and red in her hair, while also casting a warm hue to her skin. With the shadows hugging her just right, he could make out the impressive curves of her body. Her legs were slender and shapely beneath her jeans, leading up to a firmly curved backside. Her breasts tested the buttons of her shirt, straining them beneath her worn leather jacket.

Feeling his eyes upon her, Eve gave him a smile and looked back up to the sky. Her jacket was coming open to reveal a glimpse of cleavage thanks to a few unfastened shirt buttons. After all the day's commotion, her hair had almost come out of the two tails she kept it in. That made it seem even wilder as it flowed over her shoulders. The ribbons were practically lost in the soft cascade.

"I'm sorry about what happened to Emmett," Clint said.

She nodded and looked a little saddened by the words. "I didn't really know him for long. He was a good man, though."

"Something tells me he's not the first person you've lost."

Glancing over at him, Eve wore a cautious expression on her face. "Me and Vernon have worked together for a long time. We get hired to watch over folks that are in trouble. Usually, they've already gotten themselves into a pretty tight spot by the time we come into the picture. Emmett wasn't a bad sort, but he never seemed to mind that me and Vernon got shot at just so long as none of the bullets were coming his way."

"What about the claims?" Clint asked. "I thought you were out checking on those disputed claims."

"I don't think that story ever held too much water with you, Clint. Arthur might have believed it for a while, but not anymore."

"So you're after Kane?"

Studying him carefully, Eve got a somewhat playful smile on her face. Her eyes narrowed a bit and she turned so she was facing him head-on. "Kane's after us. In fact, I'd wager he's after all of us and for exactly the same reason."

Clint nodded and took a few more steps. He took note of the way Eve watched him. There wasn't so much suspicion between them anymore. Instead, there was a mutual interest to see just what the other was going to do next.

Finally, he stopped and turned toward her again. Since she'd been keeping pace with him, Eve was still less than an arm's length away. "And I'll just bet," he said while reaching out to run the backs of his fingers along her face and down the sides of her neck, "that the reason"—Clint's fingers continued down, brushing lightly against her skin as they traced along the edges of her collar—"is right here."

Clint could feel Eve's breaths quicken as his hands drew closer to the smooth slopes of her breasts. She didn't make a move to stop him, however, even when his fingers slipped underneath her shirt to pull it open a little more.

From there, Clint's fingertips found a thin gold chain around her neck and traced it between her breasts. Eve pulled in a deep breath and leaned her head back slightly as Clint gently slipped his hand into her shirt, brushing ever so close to her nipples.

When he slipped his hand out, he revealed a silver crucifix hanging from the chain. Sure enough, HOJ was inscribed on the back.

TWENTY-NINE

Eve looked down at Clint's hands. It seemed she was more disappointed in where they were than what they were holding. "Arthur's got one just like it, doesn't he?"

Clint nodded. When he lowered his gaze, he made no effort to hide the fact that he was soaking up every detail of her body before looking into her eyes once more. "He does, but you've got a hell of an advantage on him on where you keep it."

Letting out a little laugh, Eve moved forward a bit, but stopped just short of kissing him. "Then you know about why we're all out here, dodging bullets and taking on the likes of Jervis Kane. You also must know that the chances of us finding those mines go way up if we work together."

"You've got something else besides that silver cross?" Clint asked.

Nodding slowly while reaching out to take hold of Clint's hands, Eve said, "You know I do. That's how Emmett and I took to riding together. He was a lawyer in charge of my grandfather's will. I've had this cross for a while, but didn't know the half of it until Emmett came by to show me what else I was entitled to."

"One of the clues?"

Once again, Eve nodded. Her hands were around Clint's wrists and all she had to do was put them on her hips before she felt Clint's palms roaming up along her sides. "He told me about the mines and asked me to come along, seeing as how I'm already in a business that puts me around dangerous people."

Clint leaned in and let his face nestle in her hair. She smelled like the cool mountain air combined with a bit of sweetness that could only be her own scent. He could feel her body tense every now and then when his hands brushed against a sensitive spot. She was pressing against him more and more, lowering her voice to a whisper as she drew closer.

"Finding those mines would have been almost impossible for either of us," she said into Clint's ear. Her breath was hot against his skin. "If it wasn't, then only one or two clues would be enough. But if we work together, we shouldn't have much trouble."

Moving so his mouth brushed against her neck, Clint put his lips to her ear and gently bit her lobe. She drew in a quick breath and tightened her grip around his wrists. "That's a lot of trust to be putting into someone, especially with so much money involved," he said.

"We're already on the same side. And there should be plenty in those mines for the both of us."

"Still, with all the trouble surrounding these mines, I don't know if I want to throw in with someone I hardly even know."

Her hands were still around Clint's wrists as she guided him up over her body. When she felt his hands get close to her breasts, Eve moved them in until he was cupping her. Eve opened her eyes to show Clint the fire that was being stoked inside of her. "Then let's get to know each other a little better," she said.

Clint was standing with his back to a thick wall of bushes. There were rocks all around, but none of them were tall enough to offer much protection. That changed, however, when he took hold of Eve by her hips and pulled her down onto the ground. Settling down beside her, Clint nibbled on her earlobe for a bit more before moving his lips up to her waiting mouth.

Eve's breaths were strong and quick. Her hands were busy pulling open Clint's shirt and then moving on to the buckles around his waist. First, she unfastened his gun belt, and then she worked at getting his jeans down far enough for her to reach inside.

Easing his hands up underneath her shirt, Clint pulled it open so he could finally feel the bare skin of her nipples as well as the smooth curves of her breasts. He ran his hand down along her stomach and then peeled her out of her gun belt as well before sliding her jeans down over her hips.

All the while, Clint felt her hands working their way toward his groin. Her fingers were gentle, yet insistent as they found their way closer to his stiffening cock. When she got there, Eve let out a sigh and started stroking him until he started to squirm.

But Clint wasn't the only one being worked into a frenzy. He was making sure to return the favor by rubbing the slick lips of her pussy until they were wet against his fingers and Eve was opening her thighs so he could slip his fingers inside.

The disappointment was plain enough on her face when Clint moved both of his hands from where they were and onto her hips. That little frown was short-lived, however, since he pushed Eve onto her back so he could climb on top of her.

Smiling and wriggling on the ground, Eve struggled to get Clint all the way out of his jeans while lifting her hips up so he could do the same to her. Finally, she pulled one leg free and slid it along Clint's side. The other leg pushed against the ground and opened as Clint settled between them. She closed her eyes and savored the feel of his rigid cock moving against her.

Clint shifted his hips just to watch the way Eve's smile changed. When he felt himself brush against the wet, sensitive nub of her clitoris, he watched as she arched her back and grinned as though she was listening to some faraway music. He couldn't hold off much longer, however, before positioning himself just right so he could enter her with a forward thrust.

Eve's arms had slid beneath Clint's jacket and were between that and his shirt. They were both still half-dressed, which made it all the more satisfying when he started pumping between her legs. She looked up at the open sky and felt the wind move over them both. Although she wanted to let out a satisfied moan, she knew that Vernon and Arthur weren't too far away. And when she thought that way, she wanted to cry out even more.

Clint could feel the tension in her body. It was a trembling in her muscles that even worked at the muscles between her thighs. He moved one hand up and down along her bare hip, slipping under to feel her firm buttocks against the rough ground.

One of Eve's breasts was exposed and the other half of her upper body was still covered by her rumpled shirt. She still wore her jacket as well, but most of it was bunched up at the waist. As his eyes took in the sight of her hastily removed clothes hanging partially off her body, Clint savored the feeling of being inside her even more.

Eve's buttocks tensed in his hand and she strained with all her might to keep from groaning with the pleasure he was giving her. She opened her legs for him until finally both of them were wrapped around his waist. She moved her heels along his backside, pulling him in closer until his hips were pounding against her every time he thrust them forward.

After pushing all the way into her, Clint stayed where he was for a moment. He moved his hips in a slow circle, grinding against a spot that seemed to be one of Eve's favorites. He could tell immediately that he was both torturing her and bringing her to the brink of ecstasy at the same time. While she trembled with pleasure as he moved against the sweet spot he'd found, she was now making a fist in the grass next to her. It was all she could do to keep from shouting out his name at the top of her voice.

As if reacting to those thoughts within his head, a voice did make itself heard. Unfortunately, it wasn't exactly the voice that Clint had been most anxious to hear.

"Clint? Eve? Are you two over there?" Arthur shouted as his boots crunched against the fallen leaves.

Both of them froze in each other's arms. By the looks on their faces, it was hard to tell which of them wanted to kill Arthur more.

THIRTY

Arthur poked around from one set of bushes to another. He stumbled on a few branches and almost broke his neck when he started slipping down a slope covered in leaves. When he heard steps coming his way, his eyes went wide and his hand slapped against the gun still wedged under his belt.

Suddenly, Arthur's eyes grew even wider and he quickly moved his hand away from the gun.

"Settle down, Arthur," Clint said as he stepped out from behind the thick clump of bushes. "It's only us."

Arthur's breaths came in quick gulps and he was still wheezing when Eve stepped around to stand at Clint's side. "You two startled me. I wasn't sure where you went."

"Startled you?" Eve asked in a plainly aggravated tone. "You were the one calling out our names, remember?"

After thinking that over for a second, Arthur shrugged. "I guess you're right. Anyway, supper's ready. It isn't much, but it's all I could do considering what I had to work with."

Clint felt the sting of frustration with every step that he took away from the spot where he and Eve had been laying. Looking over at the way one of her ribbons had been pulled from her hair and the rumpled condition of her hastily buttoned clothes only made it worse.

"What happened to you two?" Arthur asked, apparently noticing the same things that had been distracting Clint. He nodded and snapped his fingers. "I know what happened. You slipped on some of this loose gravel, didn't you? I've almost broken my neck a few times just trying to find you both out here."

"Almost?" Eve asked sarcastically. "That's too bad." When she saw the questioning look on Arthur's face, she added, "Too bad that you almost got hurt. You said supper's ready? I'm starving."

After reaching out to squeeze Clint's backside while she was still close enough to do so without Arthur seeing, Eve jogged ahead and went back toward camp.

Clint admired the rounded curve of her behind as well as the tussled condition of her hair before turning back to look at Arthur. He jumped back a bit when he found the spindly man already closing the distance between them.

"I wanted to have a word with you about her and that other one," Arthur said.

"You mean Vernon?"

"That's the one. Anyway, he and Eve know something about the mines we're after. I'm certain of it."

Clint started to add something, but was stopped by a quickly raised hand.

"One of them might be coming back here any second," Arthur said. "Just let me finish. You might think I'm crazy here, but I think we should pool our resources. I mean, if they're after the same thing, then that means they probably have another clue.

"I've been thinking things over this whole time and I've got some notions about the two clues I have, but I haven't seen anything around us that would point us in one direction or another. Without more of these clues, we might just be wandering around for weeks. Maybe longer."

"Are you sure about this?" Clint asked.

After pondering for a few moments, Arthur began nodding. "Yes. Quite sure. I mean, if we work together, we'll have to split the money. That's better than not being able to find any of it at all. Besides," he added, pulling Clint closer even though there wasn't anyone in sight of them, "I believe there's enough in those mines to make us all richer than we could imagine. There might even be more than one stash in there."

"And what happens if we get there and those two decide to turn on us?" Clint asked, airing out something that had been in the back of his mind ever since Eve had made this same suggestion. "Large sums of money have a tendency to bring out the worst in folks."

"Yes, but that's why you're here. After what you did at that ambush, I doubt anyone would be foolish enough to cross you."

"You'd be surprised how foolish people can be."

Arthur's head lowered and his voice took on a more somber tone when he said, "Emmett was one of them and he's dead. They've both lost a good man and they're still going on. If they meant to kill us, they could have done it back then without much problem."

Despite the doubts in the back of his head, Clint had to admit that Arthur made a good point. Also, as long as he was working with him, Clint and Arthur were partners. Decisions like this one needed to be made with both partners in full agreement.

"All right then," Clint said. "Sounds like we've got a plan. In fact, I was talking to Eve before you found us and she just happens to be in the market for some new partners herself."

"Excellent. Now, we just need to convince that other one."

THIRTY-ONE

Vernon stood at the edge of the camp opposite from where Clint and Arthur would approach it. He was so still that the breeze had already buried the bottom portion of his boots in dead leaves. Branches twitched and scraped against him, but it wasn't enough to get him to budge. The only time he stirred at all was when he saw Eve hurrying toward him.

"Did you get it?" she asked.

Vernon's hand had already been buried in his pocket. When he pulled it out, he revealed what appeared to be a silver dollar. The coin was slightly larger than a dollar and even had the proper markings on one side. It was slightly thinner and had rougher edges, however, almost as though it had been heated and flattened.

"This is the first time I've gotten a close look at it," Vernon said. "That little weasel Emmett never let me near the damn thing."

"Maybe he was worried you'd steal it from his dead body," Eve said sarcastically.

Vernon smirked at that, but the expression on his face had about as much humor as the smile found on a skull. "Yeah. Maybe he was. He thought he was so damn smart, not telling us anything about what he thought this could mean. Now that I see it up close, it shouldn't be too hard to make use out of it."

When he saw Eve's eyes lingering on the coin in his hand, Vernon clamped his fingers around it and stuffed it into his pocket. "Did either of those two come after me?"

"No," Eve replied. "Arthur's been fussing around the fire cooking supper most of the time."

"What about Clint?"

"He's been busy."

"Are you sure about that?"

"Oh, yes. Real sure."

"Good," Vernon said. "Because it took me a while to find where you planted Emmett. It was worth the effort, though. This little chunk of silver puts us one step closer to being wealthy. After that, it's outlived its usefulness." With a grim smirk, he added, "Kind of like its former owner."

Eve's eyes narrowed and she scowled up at the big man. "Don't talk like that. It's disrespectful. Emmett was a good soul."

"Maybe, but are you willing to say the same for those other two we're riding with?"

"After we all nearly got killed back there, you're still not sure about Clint? He practically ran into a hornet's nest to chase those shooters away. That's enough for me."

"So you still want to bring them in with us?"

Eve nodded. "I already did." When she saw the scowl come onto Vernon's face, she added, "You knew I wanted to. We were tossing that back and forth on our way over here."

"But that still don't make it easier to swallow." After a few quiet moments, Vernon's face became as unreadable as solid rock and his eyes became colder than the chill coming down from the Rockies. "Fine. We'll ride with them for now. We'll just see how things turn out once we get to all that money."

Sounds could be heard coming from the other direction.

When Eve turned to get a look, she saw Clint and Arthur walking back into the camp. "You men and your damn treasure hunts. As much as I'd love to believe every word of it, I think I'll just wait and save my judgment until I get a look at all this gold for myself."

"You don't think there's gold?"

"I think there's something. I'll even wager there's some money or at least those old miners' nest eggs, but it would take a fool to think there's as much as everyone says there is."

"Should we lay out all our cards then?" Vernon asked.

Looking over her shoulder at him, Eve replied, "Keep that coin under your hat for now."

"For what it's worth, the only one that concerns me is the skinny one. I ain't never seen a man charge into gunfire like Clint did back there. That skinny one's too yellow for my liking. He was also too much like Emmett."

"You're not exactly joyous company either, you know," Eve chided. "Let's just see how the night goes and if we think we can still trust these two come morning, then we'll let them know it all."

Vernon nodded. The movement was so subtle it was almost like a trick of the eyes. His gaze had already locked onto the campsite and his hand hung down close to his holster. He waited until Eve had stepped into the camp before making his own presence known to the others.

THIRTY-TWO

Considering all that had happened and all that was running beneath the surface, dinner was surprisingly pleasant. Part of that might have come from the fact that they'd already toasted their new partnership over dented tin cups of coffee. Another part of that might have been that they were all too tired to fight anymore.

Once the sun had dipped below the horizon, darkness came rushing over them. Arthur wrapped himself up in an old blanket, propped himself up against a rock, and was asleep in minutes.

Vernon sat with his back to a tree. Although his eyes weren't all the way shut, his breathing was slow and steady enough to show that he was asleep. His hand lay close to his gun, twitching just enough to make waking him up too suddenly a real bad idea.

Clint's eyelids were getting heavy as well, so he kicked some dirt onto the fire and walked over to Eclipse so he could find his bedroll. Soft footsteps came up behind him, but he didn't concern himself with them. Not only did he recognize the sound, but he'd been waiting anxiously to hear it.

In one swift motion, he spun around and grabbed hold

of Eve by the waist as if he meant to pick her off her feet. She wriggled in his hands and smacked his shoulder until he let her go. When she hit the ground, she turned to get a look at the other two.

"You'll wake them," she said in a scolding whisper.

Clint was already turned back toward his saddle and removing the bedroll from where it was stored. "So? We're partners now, remember?"

Eve leaned in closer and let her lips brush against Clint's ear. "That doesn't mean I want to share everything with them. Besides, we've got some unfinished business."

"I was hoping you were thinking along those lines. Otherwise, I doubt I'd be able to get a wink of sleep."

"Well, we can't have that." With that said, she slid her arms around Clint's waist and pressed her lips against his.

Clint took her in his arms and kissed her with all the passion that had been bottled up since Arthur had interrupted them before. He broke away from her just as Eve began licking his lips and wriggling against him.

Without another word, Clint took her hand and led her away from the main camp. Although they weren't too far away, the horses and a few rocks were between them and the other two sleeping nearby. Clint spread the bedroll onto the ground, lowered himself onto it, and pulled Eve right down with him.

The moment they were laying next to each other, they slipped underneath the blanket and wrapped themselves up tight inside of it. Both Eve and Clint's hands were busy under the cover. With an urgency bordering on frantic, they struggled to get each other undressed. Buckles were unbuckled, shirts were untucked, and finally Clint felt Eve's naked skin against his own.

Trying to keep quiet, Eve let out a contented sigh. She draped one leg over Clint's side, rubbing against him as she felt his penis becoming more and more rigid. When Clint reached down to guide himself inside of her, Eve clamped her mouth onto Clint's in expectation for what was next.

As he drove his cock into her, Clint felt Eve trying to hold back a passionate scream. What she couldn't muffle on her own was kept almost to a low rustle since what little noise she made went directly into his mouth.

Clint slid his hand over her hip so he could cup her backside, guiding her as he began to pump in and out of her. They were still laying on their sides under the cover, their bodies grinding slowly against the ground as well as against each other.

After a little bit of squirming, Eve managed to get on top of Clint. She sat up with her palms flat against Clint's chest as she started riding him in a smooth rocking motion. A luxurious smile came onto her face as she arched her back and looked up at the stars scattered overhead.

Clint closed his eyes and let himself fall into the moment. He was completely enveloped by her. His hands were on her hips as she moved them back and forth. Every now and then, he moved his hands up to feel the sway of her breasts beneath her shirt.

Before too long, Clint began pumping his hips upward as she was coming down. The stronger thrusts brought an even wider smile to Eve's face as she hunkered down on top of him and let him pound up into her. Both of Clint's hands were cupping her buttocks, holding her in place.

Their bodies came together under the cover. With Eve sitting up, the cover was actually about to fall off of them. Suddenly, she snapped her eyes toward the camp. Gritting her teeth with a silent curse, she dropped down so that her face was less than an inch away from Clint's.

"Good Lord," she whispered. "I think Arthur's looking for us again."

But Clint wasn't about to be stopped so easily. Even if there was a row of cavalry officers bearing down on them, he doubted he'd be able to stop.

"Is that so?" he asked while grinding his hips against her and then driving his cock in between her legs.

Eve's breath caught in her throat and she turned her head as the beginning of her climax washed through her. "Either that . . . or Vernon." She bit down on her lip as Clint pumped into her again. "They're . . . close."

"I'm close too," Clint whispered. "In more ways that one."

"Oh, God, Clint." Although she was still tensed up, she quickly melted against him. Eve reached out with both hands to grab hold of the bedroll beneath either side of Clint's head. With her face against his, she propped up her hips so he could move more easily between them.

"Just keep going," she insisted, even though he'd never really stopped. "I don't care who finds us."

Clint grabbed hold of her and thrust his hips between her legs. The way she'd positioned herself on top of him, it seemed that his cock could push up even deeper inside of her. Finally, he was grabbing onto her buttocks and guiding her into a strong rhythm that quickly brought them both to a powerful orgasm.

Even after he'd exploded inside of her, Clint stayed where he was until the rushing sound in his ears died down a bit. When he started to move again, he felt Eve's hands squeezing his shoulders.

"Don't move," she whispered. "Stay right where you are."

Clint did as he was told, thinking that someone was either about to discover them together or that there was maybe even an animal creeping up on them. Although neither one would be too horrible, either one could make the next day's ride awkward one way or another.

But Eve wasn't worried about being found. She wasn't concerned about any animal. Instead, there was another reason for her to want Clint to stay still. Clint realized that when he felt Eve's muscles tightening and trembling around him.

The wet lips between her thighs were clenching around his rigid penis. Once he felt that, Clint knew exactly what to do. With one hand still against her rounded backside, he moved his hips gently up and down until Eve's breaths started thundering in his ear. He then pumped up into her a few more times.

His last thrust was the strongest, and it was more than enough to send her trembling body into another orgasm. After that, Eve practically melted on top of him.

"Where were you?" Arthur asked sleepily as he shifted in his spot.

Clint held up his bedroll. "Just needed to get this. Good night."

Arthur watched Clint sit down, and closed his eyes once he saw Eve step into the clearing with the rest of them.

Vernon remained where he was, shaking his head while smirking to himself.

THIRTY-THREE

The sunlight was nothing more than faint wisps in the sky. It was going to be a cold morning anyhow; that much could be felt in anyone's bones. But with the morning so young, it gave the cold a little extra bite as it sliced through the air as well as through anyone who stood in its way.

If Jervis Kane felt the cold, he didn't let on. Instead, he stood up against it as if he had something to prove. When the wind would kick up too badly, he might allow himself to scowl, but he still wouldn't back down. It was as though he had enough ice in his veins already that a little more cold wasn't about to do any damage.

"You see them?" Kane asked to one of the men around him.

The other man was the exact opposite of Kane. At least, that's how he looked. While Kane stood tall and unmoving in the early morning chill, this man was on his belly in the dirt. His chin rested on the ground and every breath he took rattled his entire body something fierce.

The man was staring through a spyglass while laying on top of a ridge. He looked down at a stretch of rugged terrain beneath him. Every so often, he would flinch as a stray bit of sunlight reflected off a frosted rock to flash into his eye. Before answering Kane's question, he took another careful look through the spyglass.

Then again, he knew better than to keep Kane waiting for much longer.

"Yeah," the man said. "I see them."

"Are they moving out yet?"

"Looks like it. I thought they were sending someone ahead of them, but it looks like they're all headed out."

"Where are they going?"

After waiting for close to a minute more, the man collapsed the spyglass and slid down from the top of the ridge. "They're headed back toward where we jumped them."

Kane nodded as though he could see the other riders himself. "Then we must've caught them near one of them landmarks."

"We're all rested up and ready to go. You want to hit them again?"

"Why bother? We're not here just to kill a woman and some gunhands. We're here to get that money and it looks like they mean to lead us a little closer toward it."

"How close you want to let them get?"

"As close as they want to take us." Kane squinted down at the man as he reached out to offer him his hand. When the man took it, Kane pulled him onto his feet. He didn't let him go just yet, however. "Why? Is something bothering you?"

"Don't you recognize who that is?"

"Who?"

"The man riding with Arthur Books."

"You mean Clint Adams?"

"Yeah," the man replied, looking somewhat confused at Kane's casual manner. "Clint Adams. He's The Gunsmith, you know."

"You think I'm stupid? Of course I know. Am I supposed to be pissing all over myself just because the man made a name for himself? I made a name for myself too. If

I'm not talked about in every saloon in the country, that just means I'm better at keeping my own business to myself."

"He could be trouble."

"He is trouble," Kane grunted. "So's Vernon and so's that bitch. That's why we'll take them all down once they don't serve no purpose. What's the matter? You scared of Clint Adams?"

The man paused before averting his eyes and muttering, "No."

"Because if you're scared of anyone, it should be me." Saying that, Kane crushed the man's hand inside his grip before knocking him back with enough force to send him to the ground. Looming over him, Kane fixed his eyes on the fallen man before glaring around at the others nearby.

"Yesterday, we tested Adams and the rest of them and damn near killed 'em all in the process. They may have guns, but we're the hunters here. Not them. They're just a bunch of ducks waiting to get plucked and once those ducks take us to where we want to go, that's just what's gonna happen."

Waiting for his words to sink in, Kane stared down each of his men in turn. Although there weren't many of them, they were scattered throughout the wooded area like an army. They all looked back at him, nodding to let Kane know they were with him.

At the right moment, Kane let a cruel smile twist his features. "And after them ducks are shot, plucked, and cooked, we'll all be rich men. By that, I mean every last goddamn one of us."

Hearing that, all of the men gathered around Kane let out a sound that was part cheer and part battle cry. The same predatory hunger that was in Kane's face now burned onto the faces of his men. They all grabbed their guns and lifted them in the air, stopping just short of firing a few shots up into the sky.

Kane liked what he saw and nodded slowly while turning toward the trail ahead. He didn't need the spyglass to see that the group he'd been watching was riding out and headed back toward the previous ambush spot. Climbing into his saddle, Kane flicked his reins and got his horse moving without looking back. He knew damn well his men would follow.

"How long do we wait?" the man with the spyglass asked.

"I'll let you know when that time comes," Kane replied. "Just be ready."

Behind him, the rest of the men scrambled to break down the rest of the camp and saddle up. They formed a staggered line of gunmen weaving in and out of the trees. Their numbers were down to five, but they were able to cover plenty of ground without drawing much attention to themselves.

As he took a path intended to circle around and intersect with the ambush site from another angle, Kane knew it would be a little while before his men got the action they were craving. Still, he knew it would be more than worth the wait.

Kane reached over his shoulder and found a small leather pouch that had been used by an Indian to carry his arrows. But rather than any arrows, this pouch now contained a bow. It was half a bow actually, carved with a design that seemed familiar, yet in a vague, maddening way.

The more he looked at it, the more frustrated Kane got. He put it away and forced his mind back onto the task at hand. He'd figure it out soon enough. All he had to do was wait.

THIRTY-FOUR

"What are we doing back here?" Arthur asked. Although it had taken him a while to realize they were headed back toward the ambush site, Arthur made up for lost time by asking that same question no fewer than ten times in a row.

Before Arthur made it an even dozen, Clint looked over to him and said, "We're in on this together now, Arthur. One of their clues points in this direction."

"Are you certain about that?"

Clint brought Eclipse to a stop. Arthur rode beside him and soon, Eve and Vernon followed suit. Shifting in his saddle, Clint looked over toward the other two. "I don't like being here any more than him. It was a good enough spot for an ambush once. There's no reason for them to pass up a chance to try it again."

"The spot we're after is a little further back," Eve said. "Before, we meant to pass it up until we could break off and circle back."

Clint waited a few moments until it seemed that she wasn't going to add anything to that. "That was then," he said. "If we're partners now, maybe it's time to let us know where we're headed before those gunmen find us again."

Eve took a deep breath as if steeling herself to take a

punch. When she let it out, she looked back to Vernon and said, "He's right. Show him what brought us here."

If Eve seemed a little reluctant, Vernon seemed downright adamant that he wasn't about to take another step forward in their newly forged partnership. Finally, he dug into his pocket. When he pulled his hand back out, it was clenched in a tight fist. He tossed the flat silver coin through the air with a quick snap of his arm before he could change his mind.

Arthur was already at Eclipse's side by the time Clint caught the coin. He stared intently, not wanting to miss the moment when Clint opened his hand to reveal what he'd been given.

"Looks like a coin," Clint said.

Eve made her way to Clint's other side. "Turn it over."

He did and found the other side to be almost completely blank. Apart from the ridges in the coin that seemed to have come when the silver was flattened, there was nothing else to see. But Clint had seen enough of the little tricks used by these old miners and figured there had to be something else that he just hadn't caught yet.

He caught it when he held the coin at an angle and watched as the light fell over the wavy contours. Squinting a bit, he studied one contour in particular before looking back to Eve.

"One of these lines was carved in here," Clint said. "It couldn't be writing, though, unless it's so worn down that there's nothing left."

"It's not writing," Eve said.

All this time, Arthur was straining to get a look at the coin. He even started reaching for it so he could pluck it from Clint's hand. When he did get to see it, Arthur glanced up and then started looking around.

Eve had been watching Arthur with amusement at first, but then she started to nod. "He's got the right idea."

Following Arthur's line of sight, Clint was able to spot

the same thing that had just caught the other man's attention. When he did, he immediately had to look back down at the coin and then back up at the horizon.

Arthur lifted a finger and pointed to a ridge roughly a few miles away. "That notch right there. The one next to that rise. It's the same shape as what's drawn on the coin."

Although Clint had been thinking the same thing, he had to look a third time to verify it. Sure enough, the one contour on the coin that seemed to have been carved into the silver was exactly the same as the contour formed by the distant horizon. Every detail was painstakingly rendered. Now that he was looking at the real ridge, Clint couldn't help but be impressed.

"Damn," Clint said in awe. "That is some fine bit of carving."

Vernon rode up a little closer to the other three. "It sure is. Emmett was given that coin by his mother, who was married to one of those miners."

"So the miner was his father?" Arthur asked.

"I guess. He didn't really talk about it and I didn't really care. Hell, I barely even believed that marking was going to mean anything until I saw it for myself."

Clint turned to face Vernon and said, "You were sure guarding it like it was your firstborn."

"Just because I don't think it's some part of a treasure map don't mean it ain't valuable. There's men willing to kill and die for it."

"Speaking of which, we shouldn't stay around here much longer."

"I agree," Eve said. "We should probably head for that notch. It's the closest thing to a landmark on that ridge."

Arthur nodded firmly. "And I concur. The landmarks should seem obvious once we're in the right spot and that's the most obvious direction."

Clint flicked his reins and turned Eclipse's nose toward the notch in the distant ridge. "Sounds good enough to me.

It'll take us a while to get there unless we stumble upon a trail that cuts through these trees. Either way, the sooner we get moving, the better."

He didn't have to say another word. Eclipse was able to find a spot to break off from the trail before too long and Clint let the stallion set his own pace. Keeping his nose down and his steps slow, the Darley Arabian eventually sniffed out the safest path and took it. Although the rocky soil shifted a bit under his feet, Eclipse quickly adjusted to it and found a gait that suited him best.

The others were right behind Clint, their horses a little more accustomed to the rugged terrain. As anxious as he was to keep moving, Arthur wound up at the back of the line. In fact, his horse seemed more willing to move forward than he did.

"Shouldn't we find a more beaten path?" Arthur asked, even though nobody seemed to be listening.

Suddenly, he heard something moving from the direction of the ambush site. Whether the sound was caused by gunmen, an animal, or even the wind, it was enough to get Arthur moving into the trees.

THIRTY-FIVE

Although rough at first, the land eased up on them once the original trail was behind them and they'd picked their way through about a quarter mile of trees. Eventually, Clint was able to find something similar enough to a path that took them in the proper direction. It wasn't much more than a wide, shallow rut in the ground, but it would have to be enough.

The terrain stretched out into a grassy field with a gentle upward slope. In the distance, the mountains loomed like a set of storm clouds. Before they reached the Rockies, however, they would make it to the ridge. Clint found himself staring at their destination, which looked as though it had been chipped out of the ridge with a giant ax.

"That's a beautiful sight," Eve said as she rode up next to him. Although the path they were taking was barely noticeable, there was enough space for two horses to ride comfortably side by side.

Clint nodded. "It'd be even better if I knew for certain that there was something at the end of this ride."

"Oh, there'll be something. There's got to be. For now, I'm just happy to see the real sight of that notch. I didn't get to see Emmett's coin too often, so I memorized every marking on it so I could look for it on my own. Good thing too, because he probably would have missed it once we got out here." Shaking her head, she added, "Poor soul. He should never have left his house."

Smirking, Clint fought the impulse to look back at Arthur riding uncomfortably next to Vernon. "We're all doing fine," he said, knowing that she was thinking about the spindly man behind them as well. "As for what might happen before this is over, we all knew the risks going in. It's safe to say that we all sure know the risks by now."

"I guess that's right. Still, you don't strike me as the treasure-hunting type. I see you as the sort who's more comfortable in a saloon than out digging for lost mines."

"I'd have to agree with you. But I'm in this far, so I might as well see it through to the end."

Eve nodded and let herself be shifted back and forth by the plodding steps of her horse. Smirking a bit, she said, "Come to think of it, I see you more at a card table in a saloon."

"What makes you say that?"

"Because you're a gambler, Clint. I can see that in your eyes. You're in this to the end because you're betting that there must be something to all this; otherwise none of these other people, or you for that matter, would be out here reading wrinkles off the back of old coins."

"While I might not have put it that way myself, I'd have to say you're probably pretty close to the truth."

Eve sat up straight in her saddle. "I know I'm right."

"Well, then, I guess that cinches it. Now, speaking of gambling," Clint added, "how about we lay all our cards on the table?"

"What do you have in mind?"

"The reason we're all here is what I have in mind. You said yourself that Emmett would have missed the landmark on his own coin. Why take that risk with the rest of us? Whatever clues we have, we should all look at now. That way we won't miss anything."

So far, Vernon had been keeping fairly quiet. When he heard those words drift back to him, however, that changed immediately. "You already got us as partners," he snarled. "Now you want it all? How are we supposed to know that you won't try to gun us down and track down them mines yourself once you've got all the clues?"

"And how am I supposed to know you won't do the same?" Clint asked. "Isn't that what being partners is all about?"

"Maybe, but only one of us is The Gunsmith. I heard enough about you and seen plenty to know that you got a hell of a good chance of dropping all of us before we knew what was going on. I'm quick on the draw myself, but I'm not about to go against someone like you."

Clint pulled back on the reins, bringing Eclipse to a stop before turning the stallion around to face Vernon. He moved up closer to the other man until Arthur was forced to move away. All the while, Clint's eyes had become cold and focused intently upon Vernon.

"I can understand why you'd be cautious," Clint said. "You'd be a fool not to. But when you talk about 'someone like me,' you're saying it like I wasn't any better than some back-shooting robber or bloodthirsty killer. I don't appreciate that kind of accusation being thrown my way. Especially when it's coming from someone I nearly took a bullet for less than a day ago."

Vernon didn't budge under Clint's harsh stare. He did, however, flinch when he heard Clint's words. He looked down a bit as though something had hit him in the stomach before looking right back into Clint's eyes again. "My apologies, Adams. That was out of line."

Staring Vernon down for another moment, Clint took the edge off his glare and nodded. "Accepted."

"I just hate to give up everything we've been guarding with our lives since this damn ride started."

"And I'd hate to drag my carcass all the way out to the base of a mountain only to find out we need to double back and ride some more just because one of us missed the turn."

There was another second or two of silence when it seemed that Vernon's features were etched in rock. Finally, the rock cracked and he let out a gruff chuckle. "You're all right, Adams. And I'll be damned if you don't make a whole lot of sense. Eve, show them the rest."

Although she was hesitant at first, seeing the easy smile that had taken over Vernon's face pushed her right through it. She reached under her jacket and felt around as though she was reaching into a series of pockets.

Before Eve's hand came back into the open, Clint looked over to Arthur. "You too," he said to the spindly man. "All the cards on the table."

"All of them?" Arthur whined.

Clint gave Arthur a stern look and replied, "Yeah, Arthur. All of them. It'll give us something to talk about as we ride."

THIRTY-SIX

The ride was slow going, but took them through country that was worth taking in piece by piece. At times, the trees offered their own beauty since they surrounded the rough path on almost every side. Leaves of every color covered the ground like a dry blanket that crunched with every one of the horses' heavy steps.

The sky had clouded over to cast a gray tint to everything beneath it, making the rocks up ahead as well as the distant mountains seem even more imposing. Although a bit daunting, the sight of those steely gray mountains had a beauty of its own. They loomed like quiet sentinels over everything even though they couldn't always be seen.

Even the air itself was restful as it brushed past Clint's ears. Most of that came from the fact that the sound of that brushing combined with the crunch of leaves under plodding hooves was all he could hear. For once, Arthur had found a task to absorb him so completely that he didn't even want to share what he'd discovered.

Eve was also just as busy as she carefully studied every line of the arrowhead and Christmas Rock that Arthur had handed to her. She held first one up and then the other, studying each one as though it alone contained every single answer she was after. Just when it seemed she was done with her examination, she would start in again.

For the first few minutes, Clint wondered what could keep her so transfixed for so long. Then, since she and Arthur were too wrapped up in their own worlds to notice much of anything else, he shrugged and turned his attention to the trail ahead. He knew to enjoy peaceful moments when they were given to him.

Besides, someone had to keep their eyes on the trail ahead of them as well as the terrain surrounding the path.

Since Clint had taken it upon himself to watch the former, Vernon decided to take the latter. While he'd seen Eve go through these motions before, Vernon seemed to be more confused by what Arthur was doing with the remaining clue that Eve had handed over.

Arthur turned the thing over and over in his hands, examining it from every angle before starting the process all over again.

After seeing that Arthur and Eve were practically going through the same motions, Vernon let out a resigned sigh and savored the peace right along with Clint. Also like Clint, Vernon didn't merely sit back and let his horse carry him along. His eyes were in constant motion, slowly watching the trees, the trail, even the sky and the path they'd left behind. Before long, he found himself taking in his surroundings with as much tenacity as Eve and Arthur were taking in whatever they held in their hands.

So far, Clint and Vernon hadn't even gotten a chance to see what the other clues were. Both men also knew better than to ask about them. Vernon figured whatever question he asked wouldn't be heard anyhow. As for Clint, he'd been around Arthur long enough to know that the man would start talking whenever he was ready. The only trick then was getting him to shut up.

As if picking up on Clint's thoughts, Arthur looked up and around until he managed to spot Eclipse at the head of the line. "What do you think about this, Clint?"

"Not much. Especially since you haven't let me see it yet."

Arthur let out a flustered laugh and flicked his reins so he could draw up next to Clint. "Of course. Here," he said, handing over the thing that Eve had dug from her pockets. "Take a look for yourself."

Accepting whatever Arthur handed over, Clint was a bit surprised by the weight of the thing. Not that it was too heavy, but it was just a lot bigger than he'd expected. The thing was slightly smaller than a cigarette case, but thick as a deck of cards. It was hollow and made from dull iron with some lead possibly mixed in, which gave it a good amount of weight.

Clint took a look at it and saw that it was carved on one side. The other side was covered with rough ridges as if something had been crudely scratched from its surface. He then turned it onto its side and saw the hinges. Using his thumb, Clint opened the metal box and looked inside to find exactly what he'd expected.

"Matches," Clint said with a shrug. "It's a match safe." Closing it so he could look more carefully at the cover, he found a simple picture of mountain scenery carved into the metal. "It looks like it could have been drawn by some miner who was bored for a few weeks."

"And that picture could very well be something right around here," Arthur added excitedly. "Look. There's the mountains. There's some woods just like the ones we've been riding through."

"To be fair, these could be mountains anywhere," Clint said. "Just because there's mountains and trees don't mean this leads to the mines we're looking for. These matches look pretty old. Maybe they've got something to do with it."

Arthur looked back to Eve. "You're certain this is meant to be used as one of the clues?"

She nodded.

"Then we should believe her." Giving her a reassuring nod, Arthur added, "I believe her."

"Great," Vernon grunted. "I know I'll sleep better tonight. What have you got there, Eve? You make anything of it?"

She held the Christmas Rock in her fingers so Vernon could see it. "I've seen it before. Well, I've seen rocks like this before. They're usually found on riverbeds and tin-panners like to keep some of the prettier ones as good-luck charms. Either that, or they give them to their little girls."

Clint had no problem picking up the wistful tone in Eve's voice when she mentioned that last part, but didn't say anything about it. Everyone had their memories and deserved to keep them for themselves.

"Anyway," Eve continued, "the green comes from some kind of moss or mold that sticks to any rocks in the water. The red is a little more rare."

"What is it?" Clint asked.

"Rust. A kind of rust anyway. I guess it could come from something in the water."

"Or something buried under the riverbed?" Arthur asked hopefully.

"I guess."

"What else have you got?" Vernon asked.

Eve held up the other item Arthur had given her and said, "It's an arrowhead, but I really don't know much about such things. It looks old, that's for certain."

"It could just be used," Clint said.

"Have you seen one like it?"

"Sure," Clint replied with a shrug. "I've ridden through Indian country plenty of times and have dealt with plenty of members from plenty of different tribes. I'm not exactly an expert on the matter, but I can tell you that arrowhead doesn't look much different than any other arrowhead I've seen. Then again, avoiding those things has usually been my policy."

"Toss it over here," Vernon grunted. "I've dealt with some redskins myself." When Eve tossed him the arrowhead, he studied it for a few seconds and looked up to find the other three staring at him expectantly. "Clint's right. This could have come from anywhere, although it definitely looks like it came from a tribe in this part of the country. Which one is hard to say.

"One thing I can say is that wherever this arrowhead was before Arthur got his hands on it, it was laying in the dirt with this side up for a good, long time." Tossing the arrowhead back to Eve, he added, "But you all probably figured that out already."

Eve kept her eyes on Vernon as she caught the arrowhead. She then flipped the piece over and compared one side to the other. "I'll be damned," she whispered, noticing that one side was bleached from the elements while the other was darker and stained by soil.

"You mean you didn't see that in all this time you were staring at the damned thing?" Vernon asked.

Looking up, Eve winced and looked back down again.

"What about you, Arthur?" When he saw the shocked and somewhat embarrassed look on the spindly man's face, Vernon chuckled to himself and shook his head. "Guess I'm good for something every now and then."

"The question now is what these things mean," Arthur said. "We've just got to trust that they all mean something because without that, we might as well go back right now."

"True," Clint interrupted. "But maybe we should go back to what Eve was saying about that rock."

Arthur waved a hand toward Clint dismissively. "We will, but my theory is that all of these clues tie together to form—"

"Yeah, but that rock," Clint cut in again. "Eve said it came from a river."

"True, but as I was saying—"

"Arthur, shut up." Before Arthur could object, Clint raised a finger and said, "Shut up and listen."

Arthur froze with his mouth still half-open. The other two seemed more amused by the way Clint had put the spindly man in his place. Before too long, however, silence fell between them. Soon, that silence was replaced by a more familiar sound.

Rushing water.

THIRTY-SEVEN

Arthur didn't say a word as they got their bearings and worked their way toward the sound of the water. Every now and then, he would mumble something to himself, but that was mostly ignored by the others in the group. Clint was used to Arthur's griping by now, and was too busy paying attention to the trail ahead to worry about his complaints.

Eclipse kept his nose down and walked steadily in the direction that Clint steered him. Even though there was no trail to speak of any longer, the Darley Arabian had enough trust in his rider to know that Clint wasn't about to make him walk anywhere that could be dangerous.

Meanwhile, Clint focused his eyes on the ground ahead to make sure that he deserved that trust as much as possible. Soon, the terrain became covered with loose rocks and was so studded with trees that Clint had to climb down from the saddle and lead Eclipse by the reins.

It became clear which of the other riders had spent more time in the rough mountain terrain. Vernon had found his way up close to Clint simply because his horse was more surefooted than the others. When he dropped down from the saddle, he landed in a subtle crouch to keep himself from slipping and breaking his leg in the process.

"Not much farther," Vernon said. After squinting so he could focus less on what he saw and more on what he heard, he nodded forward and to the right. "Should be just over that way. At least, that looks like our best bet for approaching that water from here."

Clint and Vernon kept more or less at each other's side as they wound their way between the trees and toward the increasingly louder rush of water. Once they'd gotten their footing on the uneven terrain, it became easier to maneuver. Even the horses seemed to be slipping less with every step they took.

Judging by the scraping sounds behind them, Eve and Arthur weren't too far away. In fact, a quick look in their direction showed Clint that Eve was only hanging back a ways so she could keep Arthur moving at a better pace. When she saw him glance in her direction, Eve rolled her eyes at Clint while somehow keeping herself from just letting Arthur fend for himself.

A few more steps, and Clint could see the sparkle of sunlight reflecting off the rough surface of flowing water. A couple steps after that, and Clint emerged from the trees and found himself standing at the shoulder of a stream that was about twenty feet across. One end of it extended farther than he could see. Upstream, the water ran down over a rock wall that was no more than four or five feet high.

The sight was restful and definitely pretty, but nothing too spectacular for anyone who'd spent their share of time in the mountains. For Clint, however, it was more than pretty. It was a sight for sore eyes and it was enough to make him feel the rush that must have been charging through Arthur and Eve throughout this entire search.

In fact, those two emerged from the trees not too far behind Clint and Vernon. One set of steps slowed to a halt while the others did just the opposite.

"You see that?" Vernon asked. His eyes were fixed on

something in the water and he didn't take them away when he asked the question.

Clint nodded, knowing that the gesture was mostly for himself. "Yeah," he replied. "I see it."

As soon as those words were out of Clint's mouth, he was almost knocked aside by a skinny, rushing figure. Annoyed at first, Clint looked down to see that he hadn't been pushed so much as he'd been in the way when Arthur had stumbled forward toward him.

The spindly man staggered toward the water with his eyes wide open and his arms windmilling on either side of him. Despite their wild, circular waving, those arms weren't enough to help him when Arthur finally lost his footing and dropped face-first into the water.

Clint knelt down and took hold of Arthur by one arm and the back of his shirt. "Come on, Arthur," Clint said. "Stop struggling. I've got you."

But the man kept flopping in the water the way a fish might flop around on dry land. Seeing someone wrestle with a trout under those circumstances might have been amusing. The sight of Clint wrestling with Arthur at that moment, on the other hand, was apparently downright hilarious.

Eve and Vernon broke out in laughter, which grew like wildfire the more Clint struggled. Their laughter became hysterical since, the more Clint tried to pull Arthur out of water that was only a few inches deep, the more Arthur floundered like a man drowning in the ocean.

Finally, Arthur pulled his head up and allowed himself to be yanked up like a cat being carried by the scruff of its neck. Despite the fact that he was soaking wet and already shivering in the cold, Arthur wore a smile on his face that rivaled the ones sported by Eve and Vernon.

"Glad to see you got a kick out of that," Clint said after letting Arthur go and stepping out of the water. "Next time," he said to the spindly man, "try standing up before trying to swim."

"I wasn't swimming," Arthur sputtered. "I was trying to get this." He held up the hand that had been stretched out in front of him when he was in the water. When he opened his fist, Arthur revealed a handful of rocks that were all no bigger than a nickel. Every last one of them, however, was coated in the same red and green mix as the Christmas Rock he'd been carrying with him.

"Yeah," Vernon said after taking a breath and wiping a tear from his eye. "I saw them rocks myself. It just didn't occur to me to go diving in after them. Clint saw them too, but I doubt he wanted to take a swim either."

Arthur looked down at the rocks in his hand and a frown started to form on his face.

Clint patted Arthur on the shoulder and helped him to his feet. "Actually," he said while digging in his pocket, "I wasn't looking at the rocks. I was looking at that."

Seeing that Clint was pointing to something beyond the river itself, Vernon tried to see what had caught his attention.

THIRTY-EIGHT

Unable to see anything more than the horizon and a glimpse of mountains, he looked back to Clint.

Having removed the match safe from his pocket, Clint was holding it up and comparing it to the view in front of him. His eyes darted back and forth between the carving on the match safe and the actual view of the mountains and trees beyond the stream. After a bit of shifting and subtle turning, he finally found a spot that made him smile and nod.

"There," Clint said. "That's it all right."

Vernon stepped over to Clint's side and leaned so he could get a look at the match safe for himself while standing relatively close to the man's position. Although he seemed skeptical at first, soon he was nodding just like Clint. "It sure is. Eve, you've got to take a look at this."

Eve was standing behind the men, but was in line with Clint and the scenery that had caught his attention. She didn't need to take another look at the match safe since she'd already memorized every line. "I see it," she said. "And it looks beautiful."

Still standing with the stream rushing over and around his feet, Arthur looked like a puppy that had been forgotten in the snow. He still held onto his Christmas Rocks as though waiting to get a round of applause from his audience. Finally, he stepped over to compare the carving with the actual view.

"It's a match," Arthur said in an official tone of voice. He then cracked a smile and said, "Pardon the pun."

Lowering the match safe, Clint turned around slowly to face the other three. "I think I know what these miners were thinking."

"What do you mean?" Vernon asked.

"With these clues," Clint explained. "I think I know what was on their minds when they set this up. It's like they knew where they wanted someone to start and they knew where they wanted them to end up. The only trick was to come up with a system to get them there without just writing down the directions for anyone to see.

"So far, we've just been finding spots or sights to let us know we were on the right track. But we've also been real lucky to find what we have so far. The way it was supposed to work was something like showing a path on a map using string and pins."

"There's a map?" Vernon asked.

Eve stepped forward and rested a hand on Vernon's shoulder. "No, there's not a map, but I know what Clint's saying. Think about it. If you take a map and lay it down so you can use some string to show a trail."

Clint stepped forward and picked up a Christmas Rock in one hand. "Some of these clues are the pins," he said. "They tell us we're headed in the right direction and that we're at a spot where we need to turn. Some of these other clues," he said while holding up the match safe in his other hand, "tell us which way to turn before moving on."

Slowly, Vernon started to nod. The more he absorbed what Clint was saying, the more he nodded. "That's a damn good theory."

"Actually," Arthur said as he sloshed forward, "it is a very good theory."

"I suppose you already thought of it, though, right, Arthur?" Eve asked.

Although the spindly man's first reaction seemed to be to step up and take the credit he was being offered, he soon shrank back again. "I thought of something close, but not quite the same. I'd have to say that Clint's probably got the right idea. I have heard of prospectors marking their trails on maps like that so they didn't have to draw it out for everyone to see. They guarded practically every little strike they found with their lives."

"So the gravestone was the first pin," Vernon said. "Then how come we didn't turn toward the notch on that coin way back then?"

Nobody answered right away. After a few seconds when the only sound was that of the water rushing around them, Clint finally voiced the question that nobody else really wanted to ask.

"Did anybody really check for it while we were there?"

That question was followed by another couple seconds of silence. Once the silence became thicker than the mud on Arthur's shirt, Clint said, "Didn't think so."

"You think that would have saved us some time?" Arthur asked.

The answer to that came in the form of a labored sigh from Vernon. "Let's just try to figure out where we need to go next."

THIRTY-NINE

Together, the four of them took a close look at the carving on the match safe and picked out what had to be the defining feature in the crude picture. Even though the drawing itself wasn't artistically inspired, there were enough details rendered carefully enough to show what the miners had intended to be shown.

There was a cluster of particularly tall trees that had been carved with more detail than anything else on the match safe. Since those trees were still standing in exactly the spot they were supposed to be, the four crossed the river and headed in that direction.

It was late in the afternoon and it seemed as though they'd made enough progress to fill a month of exploring. Everyone knew they had a ways to go, but still the mood among them was brighter than the sun over their heads.

Arthur was back to talking continuously about practically nothing and the others were laughing right along with him. Even Vernon seemed to be enjoying himself as they led their horses through the tangle of trees and eventually onto a path where they could ride.

The air was crisp and clean, bringing with it the scent of snow from the top of a mountain. With all of that around

him, not even Clint could help but be caught up in the spirit
of things. But as much as he tried to keep the smile on his
face, he was becoming more and more preoccupied by a
notion that was like the cold splash of water on his face.

Just as they'd figured, the clues seemed fairly simple
once they'd figured out what they were. If that was the
case, then it wasn't likely that they were much use once
each clue had served its purpose. From there, it was a short
step to realize that they only had one clue left that hadn't
been used.

If that clue was a pin in Clint's map, that left them without any idea of where to turn once they got there. So, unless that last clue brought them into the mines themselves,
they might not be smiling for very much longer.

And then there was also the knowledge that Jervis Kane
was still out there. Even though Clint had weathered a few
storms from that man, he wasn't about to declare total victory just yet. Every now and then, he would spot something
moving in the distance that was more than just a clump of
leaves or branches being pushed around by the wind.

Every so often, he would hear something like a heavy
step against the ground, but from a direction completely
different than where any of the other three were riding. He
looked, but couldn't see much of anything. At least, he
didn't see anything that made it worth his while to stop and
check on it. With so much wind, and with dry leaves, bare
branches, and animals around, there was always something
or other making noise nearby.

Clint's gut told him there was still trouble on the way,
and his brain confirmed it. After all the riding he'd done
and all the scrapes he'd gotten himself into, Clint had
learned to trust both of those things as if his life depended
on them.

Most of the time, his life was exactly what was at stake.

But now was not the time to distract everyone from what
they were doing to go chasing after shadows or random

sounds. Now was a time similar to those found in a high-stakes poker game. It was a time to wait for as long as it took before it was time to stop waiting and act.

Simple enough when he thought about it.

Following through on it, however, was another matter entirely.

Waiting was one of those things that got under a man's skin more than anything else. It was like having a moth stuck under his shirt, fluttering against his skin, yet always out of his reach. Even more maddening was the fact that there was no way to scratch the itch of waiting.

All a man could do was sit tight and let those frantic wings irritate him for as long as it took. They would stop on their own and they would not stop one moment before that no matter who that man was or how irritated he got.

Rather than wallow in those thoughts for too long, Clint tried to distract himself by joining in with the others a bit more. They were talking about where they might be headed, how much gold might be in those mines, and how Eve and Arthur had come across their own clues.

Not too surprisingly, when it came to that last subject, both of them became more distracted and less inclined to talk. They spouted on about family histories or tracking down rumors, but Clint knew better than to take all of that at face value.

In fact, when it was clear that Eve and Arthur were the ones doing practically all the talking, Clint looked over to the fourth member of the group. While Vernon had allowed himself to relax a bit around his new partners, he wasn't nearly as vocal as the other two.

Vernon rode toward the head of the group, wearing a smile on his face and a weary alertness in his eyes. Clint knew what Vernon must be thinking, since it was probably real close to the thoughts nagging at the back of his own head.

Clint even saw Vernon looking over to some of the same

random sounds that had caught his own attention. Every time he looked back to the group, Vernon seemed a little more weary.

Clint knew just how he felt.

It was getting into early evening and they were still working their way toward the landmark they'd decided on earlier. Looking up to get his bearings, Clint saw that cluster of trees looming over him as though they'd crept up on him and were about to fall on his head.

"How far do you reckon we've gone today?" Eve asked.

Arthur looked up at the sky, squinted, and nodded as though he really knew what he was doing. "I'd say at least five or six miles." Cocking his head to one side, he nodded again. "Or ten. No more than twenty, though. Wait a second. Maybe twenty, but not thirty."

Eve looked over at the spindly man with the same amused disbelief that Clint was feeling. "With all the hot air that comes out of that mouth, you should work for the railroad. I swear, Arthur, you talk so much, it's a wonder you don't get more things right."

Straightening up while wearing an offended look on his face, Arthur said, "I get plenty of things right, thank you very much. After all, I've helped us get this far, haven't I?"

"Just barely. What about you, Clint? Do you know how much ground we've covered today?"

The only reason Clint paused before answering was because he couldn't believe that someone besides Arthur could be so clueless about something so important. Sure, he might not have known down to the foot how far they'd gone, but to be completely ignorant of such things could be fatal in the wrong circumstances.

Before Clint could say anything, he saw that Vernon had already come to a stop and was even starting to climb down from his saddle. His eyes were fixed on something nearby, and he barely turned to look at the others when he spoke to them.

"I don't know exactly how far we've ridden," Vernon said. "But it's far enough."

"How do you figure?" Eve asked.

"See for yourself." With that, Vernon pointed to something just ahead of him. At first, it looked like just another clump of bare twigs poking up from the ground.

After looking closer, Clint picked out the shapes of some markers with feathers and various other items tied to them to dangle in the breeze. He climbed down from Eclipse's back and walked to where Vernon was standing.

"Whoever's got that arrowhead, bring it on over here," Vernon said. "If it was taken from somewhere in this area, this is probably the spot."

FORTY

"Leave the horses back there," Clint warned.

Both Eve and Arthur had their eyes set on the spot where Clint and Vernon were headed. They leaned forward in their saddles and moved their horses slowly toward the markers Vernon had spotted. It took a moment for Clint's words to sink in, but they finally paid attention and started climbing down.

"Better yet," Vernon added, "leave yourselves back there too."

"Oh, no," Eve retorted. "I'm not about to just stand back and let someone else take over. Not after I came this far."

"You know what this is?" Vernon asked in a voice that was bordering on a snarl. "It's an Indian burial ground. I don't know how old it is or which tribe it belongs to, but I can tell you for certain that if any redskins see us anywhere close to it, they won't be happy."

Eve snapped her head back, surprised that Vernon was talking to her like that. She then looked to Clint for support.

As much as he knew she'd hate to hear it, Clint said, "He's right. It's probably best if you stay back and let us check on it."

"So why do you get to go?" she asked.

"Yes," Arthur said. "I'd like to know that too."

Clint nodded, stepped aside, and waved toward the markers with one arm. "All right then. Be my guest. In fact, why don't we all just stomp through there and rip out some mementos while we're here? Or we can knock over what we like and piss all over the burial mounds."

Both Eve and Arthur looked equally offended.

"We would never!"

"I know that," Clint said. "But whoever tends to this burial ground doesn't. In fact, they'll probably think that we're here to do exactly those things or worse. Take a look at that arrowhead and try to convince me that whichever miner plucked that out of the ground did so with permission from the tribe that holds this land sacred."

Clint gave them a moment to soak that in. He didn't even need that long before understanding started to show in their eyes.

"Men've died for walking too close to spots like this," Vernon said. "We've already been here too long for my taste. We need to see what we need to see and be on our way. If there's trouble, whoever goes in there needs to be able to deal with it. You ready to fight off some mad-as-hell redskins, Arthur?"

The spindly man's downcast eyes and sudden lack of anything to say was plenty to answer that question.

Vernon grunted, turned his back on the others, and walked slowly toward the markers.

"Just stay here and keep an eye on him, all right?" Clint asked.

Although she didn't look happy about it, Eve nodded. "Here," she said, holding out the arrowhead. "You might need this. You're sure you don't want us there? We know what to look for and—"

"By now, we all know what to look for. If we don't find anything, I'll escort you two in there myself. Deal?"

"It's a deal."

Taking the arrowhead, Clint followed in Vernon's footsteps and entered the burial ground.

Immediately, the place had a chill about it that had nothing at all to do with the breeze. The markers were of different shapes and sizes, each one of them skillfully crafted into a symbol that went mostly beyond Clint's knowledge.

"You ever been to one of these places?" Vernon asked.

Clint watched every step he took, being extra careful not to disturb anything or attract the least bit of attention. "Not many," he replied. "For the most part, I try to steer around them if I can."

"Wise policy."

"What about you?"

"On occasion. I been to some when I was younger, and not just passing through. Me and a bunch of other stupid kids damn near got planted in one right along with the rest of the dead Injuns."

"I'll bet that cured your curiosity."

"Gave me a respect for them redskins, I can tell you that much. There was half a dozen of us young bucks and we almost got skinned by two Apaches who happened to catch us." Shaking his head, it seemed that Vernon was even more uncomfortable with being in that place.

Clint couldn't blame the man. Every step he took on that sacred ground made him feel like he was on borrowed time. The markers around him were beautiful, yet threatening at the same time. Like the markings on a wolf's coat, they were nice enough to look at, but being close enough to touch wasn't exactly a good idea.

Both men stopped talking so they could concentrate on what they were doing. Not only were they trying to keep from disturbing anything, but many of the things they saw around them could have been obscure markers themselves just as easily as they could have fallen there naturally.

On top of that, they were searching for whatever clue or landmark they needed to continue on their path.

"Here," Clint said as he stopped and squatted down. "Take a look at this, Vernon."

The man came up beside him and looked at the spot where Clint was pointing. He squinted down at the ground that was directly in front of one of the largest markers. Hunkering down even further, Vernon reached out with a tentative hand to brush aside some of the leaves that had fallen over a particular spot.

"Yep," Vernon said once the spot was clear. "That looks like it."

Both men were looking down at a ring of small rocks in the ground, not one of which was bigger than a penny. In the middle of the ring, there was an indentation filled in with something that had hardened into a mold. It was plain to see that something had been fixed to that spot with some sort of paste.

It was just as plain to see that whatever had been fixed there was missing.

"One way to be certain," Clint said. He then reached out and dropped the arrowhead into the indentation.

Apart from a few imperfections that came from time and the elements, it fit perfectly.

FORTY-ONE

"All right," Vernon said with relief as he stepped off sacred ground to where Eve and Arthur were waiting. "We've got our next pin in the map. Where to now?"

They both looked back at Vernon with wide, excited eyes.

"What did you see?" Arthur asked.

"A burial ground."

Eve nodded. "What about the arrowhead? How did that fit in?"

Clint stepped out from behind Vernon and said, "It fit in just well enough to know this is the place we're supposed to be. It pointed toward the west, so maybe that's where we're supposed to go now."

"Let's see it," Eve said as she stuck out her hand. "Maybe there's something else on there to help us."

Clint stood his ground between them and the burial site. "If there was anything else on there, you would have seen it by now. The only grooves on that arrowhead weren't put there by any tool."

"Well, maybe we can look at it one last time."

"Not anymore."

"What do you mean, Clint?" Eve asked sternly. "Where's the arrowhead?"

Arthur stepped up as well. "It belongs to me, Clint. Hand it over." Although he'd been fairly meek this entire time, Arthur managed to put a distinct edge in his voice now. That lasted right up until Clint stared him down with an even sharper edge in his eyes.

"That arrowhead is back where it belongs," Clint announced. "And it's staying there. It's served its purpose and now it's returned to its proper place. Anyone who wants to change that will have to get through me."

As Eve listened, she crossed her arms and clenched the muscles in her jaw. "That's just great. So do we just head west and hope for the best?"

"Why not?" Vernon replied. "It's just as solid as the other directions we've been treating like they was gospel."

"But there's got to be something else," Arthur pointed out. "Something more like the other clues we've found."

"Actually, the rest of you don't need to worry about that," came a voice from behind Vernon and Clint.

Eve's eyes widened and her hand dropped to the gun at her side. She stopped short of clearing leather, however, once she saw the group of men step forward to make their presence known.

Clint heard the footsteps behind him, but knew that if they were approaching that loudly, they were probably confident that they were in a good enough position to do so. Still, Clint wasn't about to stand still and let whoever it was stick a gun in his back, so he stepped forward while twisting around to see what was going on.

Vernon made a similar move, but wasn't quick enough to avoid feeling the cold touch of iron against his ribs.

"Everyone just mind yer manners and you might live through the day. After all, it's the least I can do considering you brought me close enough to smell the gold in them mines." As he said that, Jervis Kane entered the burial grounds from the opposite end with two of his men.

All of them had their guns drawn.

FORTY-TWO

The men all stepped out at once. Kane and two others were directly behind Clint, while another three emerged from the surrounding trees just enough to be seen. There were a few rifles in the bunch, but most of the irons in hand were pistols.

"You're real good at hiding," Vernon said. "I'm just surprised you didn't keep hiding and let your men come out here to deal with us for you."

"And why would I do that?" Kane asked. "You four seemed to be doing your jobs so well that I thought you should get a good look at who you've really been working for."

Kane was a big man. He stood several inches taller than Clint, and filled out his buckskins and battered denim as though the clothes had been draped around a barrel. The pistol he carried was rare among most gunfighters simply because it was too bulky to be drawn with much speed. In his pawlike hand, however, it seemed to be right at home.

"Actually," Kane said, "I do owe you some thanks. Listening in on your conversations has been the best schooling I've ever had. Because of that, I was able to take this and pick out where I needed to go in no time at all."

When he said that, Kane held up the broken bow he'd been carrying with him the entire time. He showed it to Clint and the others like a proud child displaying his first effort at whittling. Easing it back into the leather holder slung over his shoulder, he went on to say, "Of course, now that I'm here, I don't reckon I'll be needing your services any longer."

"Those mines really must be close," Eve said. "Because I'll just bet you couldn't find your own ass with a funnel."

Kane's mouth twitched, but it was more of a wicked smile than any sort of anger at what Eve had said. He walked forward and reached out for her chin, only to be slapped away the moment he touched her.

"Oh, you got fire," Kane mused. "I like that. Maybe I'll keep you alive so's we can celebrate once we get that gold. Of course, that really ain't necessary, since all I need to do is make sure we bring that pretty little body of yours along with us."

"You got what you wanted, Kane," Clint said. "Just take it and go."

Allowing his eyes to linger on Eve for a few more moments, Kane shook his head. "It don't work like that. Not while you got them guns on. Toss yer weapons and maybe then we can bargain."

Clint looked around at the men surrounding them. Not only were they all brandishing their weapons, but the men had already spread out to form a firing line. Their eyes were cold and merciless, as if their triggers were as good as pulled and the blood was already on their hands.

"There still may be some things I don't know about them mines," Kane said. "Seein' as how I ain't properly related to any of them old coots who found 'em. Fill me in on your family history and I might see my way clear to letting you loose."

Vernon's eyes were burning slits. His jaw was clenched

shut and his hand curled into a fist over his gun. From where he was standing, Clint could hear the breaths churning inside Vernon's lungs.

"You think you can find the mines?" Clint asked. "Then go find them yourself. If you needed any more help, I doubt you'd be so lackadaisical about it."

"Maybe I'm a kind soul."

"This is the first time I've ever really talked to you," Clint said, "and I already know that's a line of bullshit."

"You mean to kill us, Kane," Eve said. "Either get to it, or shut up. I'm sick of looking at your face."

Kane remained where he was, maintaining his position right down to the downward slant of his head. His eyes looked simple in a way, and his face looked like that of a big, mean-spirited kid who was born bad with nowhere else to go from there.

When he smiled, Kane showed a row of large, crooked teeth that made his mouth look like a poorly tended graveyard. "Guess I never was much of an actor. I do mean it when I say thank you for all you done. I never would've found this gold without you."

Kane stepped back a few paces until he was about as far back as the rest of his men. Now, his group formed a semicircle around Clint, Eve, Vernon, and Arthur. The latter group still hadn't relinquished their weapons, but judging by the look in the eyes of the former group, that didn't really matter much.

"Tell you what," Clint said. "Since you've got one of the clues, we're willing to split whatever's in those mines with you."

Eve started to voice her disagreement with that idea, but was actually stopped by Vernon.

Clint went on to add, "It's only fair and there should be plenty in there to go around, right?"

For a moment, it actually seemed as if Kane was thinking that over. When that moment passed, he shook his head. "Splitting it with my own men is cutting our shares down enough. Splitting it four more ways besides just ain't going to happen." To his men, he barked, "Kill 'em."

FORTY-THREE

When Kane gave his order, Clint didn't hear exactly what was said. All he concerned himself with was that it was too late to bargain or talk and it was time to fight for his life.

Since he couldn't look in every direction at once, Clint took a gamble that Vernon could hold his own for the first few moments. Standing with his back to Vernon, Clint focused his eyes on Kane and the men standing on either side of him.

The first one to fire was the man to Kane's left, and he did so from the hip. He managed to get his shot off before anyone else because Clint was more concerned about the man to Kane's right. That one was actually lifting his gun to take aim, which made him more of a threat.

Sure enough, the first man to fire was also the first one to miss. His round came close, but only managed to rip through the bottom part of Arthur's jacket while scraping a bit of his skin.

The man in Clint's sights was able to pick a target and sight down the barrel before the fight truly got under way.

Clint's hand flashed down to his side and snapped back up again holding the modified Colt. The pistol fit so easily in his grip that it was like an extension of his own flesh and blood. Aiming as if he was pointing his finger, Clint pulled his trigger and sent a bullet straight through the gunman's heart.

Staggering back as though he'd been kicked in the chest, the man on Kane's right pulled his trigger as every muscle in his body clenched. He fell onto his back and stayed there, twitching a few times before going limp.

Arthur dropped to the ground before he realized he'd been grazed by a bullet. When he saw the blood on his hands, he curled up into a ball and covered his head with both hands.

Shots exploded from behind Clint, but he knew that it wouldn't do him any good to worry about them. Sure enough, he soon heard more shots coming from what had to be Eve's or Vernon's weapons.

Kane's remaining three gunmen were staggered around the tree line in front of Vernon and Eve. Two of them were closer to Vernon while one was practically staring directly into Eve's face. Among them, the first to fire was one of the two closest to Vernon. The other gunman in Vernon's sights wasn't too far behind his partner, however, and their shots added to the thunder filling the air.

Vernon felt a pinch against his side, followed by a fiery heat flowing through his ribs. Reflexively grabbing hold of his wounded side with his free arm, Vernon dropped to one knee as two more shots blazed past him. As soon as his knee hit the ground, he pulled his trigger twice in quick succession.

Smoke plumed in front of him, mixing with the rest that had spewed from the other guns to turn the air into a murky soup. Despite the gritty texture fogging his vision, Vernon saw one of the gunmen stagger and grunt in pain. He used that to focus his aim even more and pulled his trigger once more.

This time, the only thing Vernon heard was the wet slap

of lead punching through flesh. That was quickly followed by a heavy thump of a body hitting the dirt.

Standing with her back to the rest of her partners, Eve felt as though the last few seconds had ticked by like hours. In that short span of time, she saw the gunman in front of her wince slightly before bringing his shotgun up to fire.

The shotgunner seemed to be aiming for Arthur at first, but couldn't get a clear shot since the spindly man had all but disappeared from sight. He shifted his aim toward Eve, pausing for an instant before sealing the woman's fate.

That brief pause was all Eve needed to draw her gun. When she took aim, she took a step forward to be sure not to miss. Eve was staring directly into the shotgunner's face as she jammed her gun's barrel into the man's gut and pulled her trigger.

Each one of her shots sounded with a muffled thump. Each time she pulled her trigger, the shotgunner jerked up off the ground. His eyes were wide with disbelief, until they finally glazed over as Eve's fourth shot exploded out through his back.

As the shotgunner dropped over, Eve was close behind him. She dived for cover, snatching up the shotgun before rolling around to get a look at the rest of the chaos around her.

Clint had shifted a bit where he stood, but kept his feet planted. No matter how much lead hissed through the air or how much blood spilled around him, the expression on his face remained as cool as the mountain air. His eyes squinted every now and then, but that was just to adjust to the churning black smoke being spat out from the gun barrels surrounding him.

Kane was gritting his teeth and opening his mouth to shout something that was lost amid the roar of gunfire that had descended upon them like a hellish storm. He'd brought his gun up to fire, but was forced to pull back when Clint fired a round in his direction.

Although he knew he would probably miss with the quickly fired round, all Clint meant to do was put Kane in check for another second or two. The moment he saw that he'd succeeded on that front, he turned his attention back to the man on Kane's left.

That gunman had fired a few more rounds into the group as a whole. Once he got a solid grip on his pistol, he held it low and fanned the hammer. The cylinder emptied in an impressive, clattering roar. One last roar sounded, but it didn't come from the gun in that man's hand.

That shot had come from Clint's Colt and, while not as furious as the previous display, it accomplished what all the sound and fury hadn't. Clint's round drilled a hole through the gunman's head, snapping him onto his back like a hinged target in a shooting gallery.

Although he knew Kane was on the move, Clint saw something that was enough to make him turn away from the bigger man.

Vernon was still on one knee, but was now hunched forward and hacking loudly to try and pull in a breath. He gripped his gun in a trembling hand and when he looked up, he displayed a face covered in blood and pink foam.

Clint saw the last remaining gunman stepping forward to place his gun to Vernon's temple. When Vernon didn't immediately react, Clint twisted on the balls of his feet and fired one shot that caught the gunman in the chest.

It staggered the man, but not enough to drop him. Clint's next shot finished the job, punching the gunman in the chest and dropping him backward onto the ground.

Even as he hit the dirt, however, the gunman's finger had been squeezing his trigger. All he needed was another trickle of strength to drop his hammer. The gunman managed that with his dying breath. The pistol bucked in his hand and was dropped a second later.

Even as he saw Vernon topple to the ground, Clint turned away from him to face Kane. The bigger man was already sighting down his barrel and just about to pull his trigger when another shot cracked through the air.

This shot came from so close to him that Clint jumped reflexively at its sound. He saw Kane twitch as a piece of his leg was chipped away by the passing bullet, but that wasn't enough to put an end to it. Kane let out an animal's snarl as he dredged up whatever he had left so he could take his shot at Clint.

Before Kane could pull his trigger, Clint brought around his Colt and sent a round through Kane's eye. The impact snapped Kane's head to one side and sent him twisting around on one foot as if in some kind of gruesome dance.

The dance ended with Kane hanging in an awkward position for a fraction of a second and then collapsing into a heap.

Only then did Clint look around to see who'd fired the shot right before his own. To his surprise, he found Arthur still huddled in a ball but pointing a smoking pistol in Kane's direction. Going by the look on Arthur's face, he was more surprised than anybody at his timing and marksmanship.

FORTY-FOUR

Still holding onto his Colt, Clint surveyed the area for any other signs of danger. The only thing moving was the smoke curling through the air like wispy serpents riding the breeze.

"You all right, Arthur?" Clint asked, extending a hand toward the spindly man.

Arthur was still trembling and too shaken to even see that Clint was trying to help get him to his feet. "I d-don't quite know."

"What about you, Eve? Are you hit?"

"I caught a few nicks and scratches, but I'm all right," she replied. "What about you?"

Clint didn't respond. He was too busy crouching down by Vernon, who was on both knees and crumpled over as though he'd been kicked in the stomach.

"Easy there, partner," Clint said. "Let's get a look at you."

Vernon tried to speak, but could only get out a strained wheeze. Although he allowed himself to be guided by Clint's hand on his shoulder, Vernon was no longer able to keep himself upright. His legs buckled from underneath him and he dropped over to one side.

Clint had no trouble catching him, and eased him onto the ground before rolling him onto his back. The first thing he saw was the pink foam that had erupted from his mouth to coat the bottom part of his face. The next thing he saw was the dark hole in Vernon's chest.

"Oh, Lord," Eve said as she rushed over to Vernon's side. "Is he . . . ?"

"Looks like he got shot through a lung," Clint said.

Vernon looked at them both, tried to suck in one more breath, and then let it out with a powerful shudder.

"Vernon?" Eve grabbed the man's shoulder. "Vernon!"

Shaking his head, Clint lowered Vernon down so he was laying all the way back with his head on the ground. After that, Clint reached out and closed the big man's eyes.

"Is he dead?" said Arthur's hesitant voice from behind them.

"Yeah, Arthur," Clint replied. "He's gone."

Eve didn't say another word. Although tears streamed down her face, she didn't allow herself to break down or even sob out loud. Instead, she stood up, walked over to the dead man who'd finished Vernon off, and emptied her gun into the corpse.

Those last few shots punched through the air with a different power than the ones that had come before. Each one was like a hammer against rock, rolling through the air even after Eve's bullets were all spent.

While refilling her pistol, Eve walked over to where Kane was laying. She put one more round into him and then knelt down next to the body.

"Are there any more of them?" Arthur asked.

Clint stood up and looked around. "I doubt it. They would have made their move already. If there were any left, they probably turned and ran by now."

"What if they didn't?"

"Then they'll have to take the same chance that these other men did. What are you doing over there, Eve?"

She stood up and held the broken bow that Kane had been carrying so they could all see it. "Here, Arthur," she said while tossing it toward him. "See what you can make of this."

Arthur's hands were still trembling, but he managed to catch the bow all the same. He turned it over a few times while quickly looking the piece of wood up and down. Finally, he pulled in a calming breath and studied the bow more carefully.

"I see it now," Arthur said. "There's a carving." He held it in front of him and turned in a slow circle. Shaking his head, he said, "it looks like it could be pointing us somewhere, but I can't exactly tell where."

Clint walked toward the burial ground and pulled Arthur along with him. "Come on. I'll take you to where the arrowhead is. Maybe that's where you need to be to see whatever you need to see."

Arthur was more than happy to get away from the smoky clearing and the bodies scattered all over the ground. When he got to the spot where Clint had replaced the arrowhead, he held up the bow one more time and made his slow circle while surveying the area.

He barely turned a quarter of the way around before stopping and nodding. "This is it," Arthur said.

Clint stepped up behind him and looked over Arthur's shoulder. There were markings carved onto the bow. They weren't as detailed as the ones on the match safe still in Clint's pocket, but were a little better than the ones on the silver coin. This time, there was a ridge drawn onto the bow with a small X carved into a particular spot.

"You think that's the entrance to the mines?" Arthur asked.

"It better be," Clint said. "Unless there's someone else following us, we're fresh out of pins."

FORTY-FIVE

The burial grounds had one more resident by the time Clint, Eve, and Arthur rode away from them. Vernon was buried in a secluded spot that didn't encroach on the Indian markers, but was close enough to share in the blessings bestowed on them.

The ride toward the spot marked on Kane's bow was short and quiet. Clint led the way as they picked through the trees and into increasingly rougher terrain. As near as they could tell, the X on the bow marked a spot at the base of a small ridge in the distance. After the ground sloped sharply downward, that ridge disappeared from view.

A minute or so later, Clint squinted at a spot no more than twenty yards ahead. "Eve, come here. Take a look at this."

She'd been keeping to herself since scooping the last bit of dirt onto Vernon, and had lagged well behind the other two ever since. Moving up to where Clint waited, she stared out in the direction he was pointing. Soon, she got a spark in her eye while leaning forward in her saddle.

"I'll be damned," she whispered.

Arthur rode up beside them like an excited kid trying to

look over their shoulders. "What is it? What are you two looking at?"

But Arthur didn't need anyone to answer those questions. As soon as he looked where Clint and Eve were looking, he saw exactly what had captured their attention.

Nestled in a thick tangle of orange and dark red bushes and covered in a thick blanket of dead leaves, there was a large frame made out of old timber that leaned precariously to one side. The frame was less than five feet high and appeared to have fallen in on itself at least once already. The opening was still barely visible, however, and it was a yawning black hole that led into the side of a hill.

"Could that be it?" Eve asked.

Clint nodded. "That's about where we were pointed. And it sure looks like it's well hidden enough to warrant a hunt like this one."

"That is it," Arthur stated. "I know it."

Before anyone could say anything else, Arthur snapped his reins and rode toward the leaning frame. Clint and Eve were close behind, and soon all three of them were climbing down from their saddles so they could continue on foot.

They reached the frame after twenty minutes or so of picking their way through the undergrowth. Plenty of the branches and obstructions in their path had obviously been tossed there on purpose. That only made Clint more confident that they'd finally reached the end of their search.

Once they reached the leaning frame, they only stopped long enough to put together a few crude torches, light them, and move on. The flickering light from the torches illuminated the narrow tunnel beyond the frame. Clint was the first one to enter, and Arthur pushed anxiously in after him. Eve brought up the rear, carefully looking at every little dust-covered shape she could find.

"Looks like there were miners here," she said. "There's picks and shovels all over the place."

"Plenty of broken lanterns too," Clint added. "By the looks of it, they lived in here for a while as well. There's a spot here where a few campfires were built and there's some pots and pans close to it."

"This is it," Arthur said excitedly. "This is definitely it."

"Could be," Clint said. "But there's only one problem."

"What problem?" Eve asked.

Having already come to a stop about thirty feet into the cave, Clint was crouching down with his head and shoulders scraping against the rocky ceiling. Turning to look at the others, he stepped aside to reveal a solid wall of rock, broken wood, and dirt. Even the cracks between some of the rocks had filled in with mud and frozen over several times over the years.

"No," Eve said as she pushed Arthur aside and ran to the wall. After dropping her torch, she pressed both hands on the wall and pushed against it with all her might. "No!" she screamed. Her voice echoed in the confined space, soon to be followed by the thump of her fists, shoulders, and feet against the wall.

Arthur was standing at the edge of the wall on the side opposite from Clint. He was feeling along the line where the rocks met up with the stone that formed the cave itself. Every so often, he could push in a finger up to the first knuckle, but could never get any farther than that. He looked over to Clint wearing a forlorn expression and shook his head.

Eve, on the other hand, wasn't going to give up so easily. "This can't be," she said. "After coming all this way, this can't be all there is." Each word sounded fiercer than the last. Still slamming her fists against the wall, the only thing she accomplished was loosening a few trickles of dust while bloodying her knuckles.

Having already stepped back from the wall, Clint was searching among the debris the miners had left behind. "One thing's for certain," he said. "There was definitely a lot more in here. By the looks of it, they stayed here for a least a week. Maybe more. And they did plenty of work while they were here."

Arthur was on his knees, scraping his hand against the wall closer to the ground. "I agree. There's ruts in the ground from a cart leading past this wall."

"We need to tear this down," Eve said breathlessly.

Arthur reached up to her and put a hand on her arm. "No," he said. Holding up fingers covered with a fuzzy green substance, he asked, "See this? There's enough moss growing down here to make a garden. Some of this wood's even started to petrify."

Yanking her arm away from him, Eve snarled, "So what?"

"That means this wall's been here for a long time. I'd even wager it was here when the miners who sent those clues got here."

"What about the cart tracks?" Eve asked. "What about the tools?"

Clint was pushing aside a pile of dirt, scooping away rubbish and rocks until he found something else and dusted it off. "There was a mine here," he said. "At least, there was a mine somewhere around here."

"Well, we won't be able to find it. Not unless we want to spend the rest of our lives searching for it."

"Now we see why the old miners needed to set up their base camp," Arthur said. "They meant to search for it as well."

"But they had to find something to get them started," Clint said. "And I think I know what it was." Saying that, Clint stood up and lifted a saddlebag out from where it had been buried. It was heavy enough to bring a smile to his face. "I get the feeling this trip wasn't exactly wasted."

FORTY-SIX

The saddlebag was filled with gold nuggets as well as a few rough gemstones. And, confirming the miners' claim to having left something for their families, there were five saddlebags in all.

"Not quite what the legend had built it up to be," Clint said. "But more than enough to make this trip worthwhile."

"Load them onto my horse," Eve said. "It's used to hauling loads heavier than that."

"You sure about that?" Clint asked while glancing out at where Eve's horse was grazing. "It's a long way back."

"Yeah, Clint. I'm sure." Punctuating that statement, there came the metallic click of a pistol's hammer being cocked back.

Clint turned around to look at her, and saw that Eve was walking straight toward him so she could stick the barrel of her gun into his ribs. It was too late for him to draw his own gun and the cave was too cramped to get away from her.

"This has been hard on all of us, Eve," Clint said. "Don't make it worse."

"I came into this expecting to find a fortune. I lost a good friend along the way. I won't leave here without getting everything I'm due."

"How do you expect to get out of here?" Clint asked.

Looking over to Arthur, Eve said, "Pitch your gun away." When the spindly man did as he was told, she said, "Now come over here and take Clint's."

Again, Arthur did as he was told.

"Now hand me some of that rope."

Twenty minutes later, Arthur and Clint were tied with their backs to one another just inside the leaning frame of the entrance. Two of the saddlebags were on Eve's horse and another two were on Arthur's. She climbed into her saddle, still holding the reins to Arthur's horse.

"I left you a little bit of play in the ropes tying your hands," she said. "There's not much, but you should be able to work your way free in a few hours. It'll take you a while to get your feet untied, though, even with both hands to work with."

Clint squirmed in his ropes and guessed that she was probably right.

"You two are both good men," she said. "That's why I'm not going to kill you."

"What about the next time we meet up?" Clint asked.

"Well, that'll be different. I left one of those bags for you, so there's no reason for hard feelings. Believe me, Vernon would have played this out in a way that would've been a lot worse for the both of you."

Glaring up into her eyes, Clint said, "I doubt that."

Eve shrugged. "No matter. This is the way it's gonna go." Smirking, she added, "Why do you think my grand-daddy called the start of this hunt Scorpion's Tail?"

"Because someone was bound to get stung."

Tipping her hat, Eve smiled and blew Clint a kiss. "It was great riding with you, Clint. You gave me one hell of a ride."

With that, Eve flicked her reins and got both of her horses moving. Once they'd cleared the branches and thick carpet of dead leaves, the horses broke into a run, leaving Clint, Arthur, and the empty cave behind them.

Just over an hour later, Clint got one of his hands free from his ropes. It only took another couple minutes after that before both he and Arthur were standing up and working the kinks out of their aching joints.

"I swear to God, Arthur," Clint grumbled. "By the way you helped out, I'd almost swear you were on Eve's side."

"I just wanted her to leave," the spindly man said.

Clint shook his head, forcing himself to be quiet until he was standing and completely out of the ropes. "Let's just get out of here, Arthur. At least we've got a bit of profit out of all this."

"Oh, we'll have more than that."

Looking over, Clint saw that Arthur was once again crawling along the base of the collapsed wall. "What are you doing over there?"

"Just following up on a hunch." Arthur kept digging at the bottom of the wall with his hands. "I found something earlier, but didn't get to say anything about it before Eve made her move."

Saying that, Arthur moved aside and let Clint get in closer. What he'd uncovered resembled a coil of thick string. One end was at the top of the coil and the other was beneath the collapsed wall itself.

"When I saw this, I was reminded of one of the other clues," Arthur said. "The more I thought about it, the more I knew it would probably be worth our while to let Eve take whatever was left in plain sight and be on her way."

Clint looked down at the coil of string and then back to Arthur. For the first time since the trip had started, every word Arthur said made perfect sense.

Just to be certain, Clint knelt down and got a look at the string for himself. Sure enough, it wasn't string.

"Got a match?" Arthur asked.

Clint dug the match safe from his pocket, removed one of the matches, and struck it against the wall. He then reached out and touched the flame to the end of the coil. After a few moments, the spark caught and started working its way down along the coil.

As much as Arthur wanted to stand there and watch, Clint dragged him out of the cave and out a ways past the frame. There was a muffled explosion that shook the ground, caused some dirt to fall at the opening of the cave, and started a small cascade of rocks inside.

Waving away the smoke and dust, Clint and Arthur walked into the cave. Amazingly enough, the tunnel was still there. The explosion had been just big enough to knock a chunk out of the collapsed wall. When he pulled out some of the larger pieces and set them aside, Clint was able to step past the wall and into a larger chamber that opened into an even deeper mine shaft.

But there was no need to walk any further. Clint was already looking at enough gold nuggets piled throughout the room to cast a sparkling glimmer using just the stray beams of light that made their way in from the outside.

"What's in there, Clint?" Arthur asked as he struggled to climb over the broken rocks without breaking his neck. "Was I right?"

Clint didn't look over his shoulder. Even if he'd wanted to, he simply couldn't have looked away from all that gold. "I never thought I'd say this, Arthur, but you're a genius."

Watch for

INNOCENT BLOOD

285th novel in the exciting GUNSMITH series

from Jove

Coming in September!

J. R. ROBERTS
THE GUNSMITH

Available wherever books are sold or at
penguin.com

(Ad # B11B)